Could It Always Be This Way,

or were they destined to live in different worlds?

He held her away from him and looked down at her with love-glazed eyes. "Silken fire and flame," he whispered. "I want to make love to you every day of my life. I want yours to be the first face I see when I wake in the morning. Whenever I reach out to you I want you to be there for me." He smoothed the red hair away from her face. "Maybe you're right, April. Maybe I am a Latin chauvinist. And that's not going to change. I'm not going to change. Love me as I am, because you're a part of me now."

It was the voice of the real world—and it terrified her.

Dear Reader:

Silhouette has always tried to give you exactly what you want. When you asked for increased realism, deeper characterization and greater length, we brought you Silhouette Special Editions. When you asked for increased sensuality, we brought you Silhouette Desire. Now you ask for books with the length and depth of Special Editions, the sensuality of Desire, but with something else besides, something that no one else offers. Now we bring you SILHOUETTE INTIMATE MOMENTS, true romance novels, longer than the usual, with all the depth that length requires. More sensuous than the usual, with characters whose maturity matches that sensuality. Books with the ingredient no one else has tapped: excitement.

There is an electricity between two people in love that makes everything they do magic, larger than life—and this is what we bring you in SILHOUETTE INTIMATE MOMENTS. Look for them wherever you buy books.

These books are for the woman who wants more than she has ever had before. These books are for you. As always, we look forward to your comments and suggestions. You can write to me at the address below:

Karen Solem
Editor-in-Chief
Silhouette Books
P.O. Box 769
New York, N.Y. 10019

The Promise of Summer

Barbara Faith

Silhouette Intimate Moments
Published by Silhouette Books New York
America's Publisher of Contemporary Romance

SILHOUETTE BOOKS, a Division of Simon & Schuster, Inc.
1230 Avenue of the Americas, New York, N.Y. 10020

ISBN: 0-671-47123-6

First Silhouette Books printing August, 1983

10 9 8 7 6 5 4 3 2 1

America's Publisher of Contemporary Romance

Printed in the U.S.A.

For Nataleigh

Chapter 1

"OLÉ!" THE WORD, AT FIRST ONLY A MUTED SOUND OF approval, rose in intensity like the fast chugging of a train leaving the station. *"Olé! . . . Olé! . . . Olé!"* Faster, faster, louder, louder. The word burst forth from thousands of throats until the arena exploded in a scream of excitement.

April Juneau found herself on her feet with the rest of them, shouting as the others shouted, waving her broad-brimmed pink straw hat as she called, *"Bravo, Matador! Bravo!"*

Beside her, Esteban grinned and said, "Now, what do you think of my cousin?"

"He's magnificent!"

And he was. She'd been to a lot of bullfights and seen a lot of matadors that year, which she'd spent in Spain, but never one to equal Alejandro Cervantes, this man who moved with sensual grace, who held his body as though the blood of kings flowed through his veins, whose arrogant face defied death as he called the monster of a bull closer and yet closer.

His feet barely moved as the animal passed him on his right side. The red cape swirled in the hot Spanish sun. The bull moved closer to him as he called to it in a strangely seductive voice: *"Toro, ahaa, Toro!"* Turning to face it, his body exposed, his stomach and groin on a level with the sharp white horns, he whispered, *"Venga!* Come, come and get me!"

April's palms were damp. Beside her, Esteban murmured, "That's enough, Alec, enough," and sucked in his breath in a gasp of fear as the bull lunged so close to the man's body that his satin suit was smeared by the blood from the wound that the picador had made.

Again and again, pass after pass. Sometimes on his knees, the cape swirling over his head as the bull swept past. Now standing as he executed right-handed *derechazos,* ending the series with a *remate,* a finishing flourish that drew applause. Then a series of left-handed *naturales,* facing the bull with the sword in his right hand, held at his side as he provoked the charge, swaying with the attack, moving the cloth in a smooth swing ahead of the bull, pulling the animal past his body in a quarter circle.

When it was time for the kill, he did it quickly and cleanly and was awarded two ears and a tail.

As he made a circle of the ring the jubilant crowd showered him with bouquets and *botas* of wine. Because this was his last bull of the day, he tilted his head back and drank from several of the *botas.*

Straw hats sailed into the ring, and either Alejandro or one of his men threw them back. April laughed as a woman's high-heeled sandal flew through the air. Cervantes picked it up, touched it to his lips, then tossed it back to the woman.

This Alejandro Cervantes was quite a man, April

thought. He certainly knew how to please a crowd—especially the women.

He was taller than most of the matadors she'd seen, and a bit broader about the shoulders. His body was sleek and trim, and the silver-encrusted black satin suit of lights that he wore looked as though it had been painted on him. Though he and Esteban were cousins, they did not look alike at all, for the man beside her was fair, and this man, pausing now under the *barrera* where they sat, was dark-skinned. There was a Gypsy look about him, and she could see when he looked up at them that his eyes were Gypsy green.

"*Bravo!*" Esteban called. "*Bravo, Matador!*"

April, as excited as everyone else, clapped her hands and, almost without thinking, flung her pink straw hat into the ring.

Cervantes caught it before it hit the sand. With a half-smile he touched his lips to the edge of the broad brim, but as she waited expectantly for him to throw it back up to her, he turned away and walked to the center of the ring, her hat still clutched in his hand, to take his final bow.

"My hat!" she said indignantly. "He's got my new hat!"

Esteban chuckled. "You'll get it back. Don't worry."

"Don't worry? It's new. I looked all over Madrid for it. Look, I know Alejandro's your cousin, but . . ."

"We're going to stop in at his place for a drink later. I think he kept your hat to make sure you'd show up."

"If he ruins it, I'll kill him," April said, laughing in spite of herself. "It's a perfect match for my dress."

Both dress and hat were pale pink, a shade that added a glow of color to her fair skin and was a perfect complement to her auburn hair. The top of the dress was silk chiffon. The short sleeves were ruffled and so was the low V-plunge neckline, which hid with its soft folds the full rise of her breasts. The skirt and matching jacket were of a soft wool material.

"Stop frowning," Esteban chided as he took her arm to lead her out of the plaza.

"All right, *amigo.*" She reached over and patted his arm. She was fond of Esteban. He was a good-looking man, totally charming and wild about sport cars, but he had absolutely no sense of time and opportunity passing him by. To April's way of thinking, he lacked ambition. Although he had been offered an executive position in the home office of the wine company that employed them both, he preferred to oversee the work in the vineyards instead. He loved the planting, nurturing and harvesting of the grapes. He didn't mind mud-caked shoes or a sweaty shirt sticking to his back. The time that he had to spend in the office grated on his nerves, and April thought that he would continue to turn down the offer of an office with his name on the door.

But she understood how he felt about the vineyards. Born in the Napa Valley region of California, April had grown up listening to her father and uncles talk of nothing except the year's grape crop and the quality of wine it would produce. From the time she was twelve she spent her summers working in the family vineyards, the plant, or the office. When she was twenty-one she graduated from the University of California at Santa Barbara with a major in business administration and a minor in Spanish literature.

Things changed while April was away at college. Her father had semiretired by the time she returned home, and her Uncle André's two sons were running things. They were willing to make a place for her, but she

decided it was time to get out on her own. When the
famous Spanish wine company Bodegas de Torreblanca
offered her a job in its New York office, she'd taken it.
She'd risen rapidly, and they'd sent her to Madrid to
learn more about the operation of the company.

.After a year there, she now felt at home in Madrid.
She missed her old friends, but she'd made new ones
and developed new interests. She loved the bullfights
and had gone every Sunday since the season began.
There had been many good matadors, but none, she
knew, as good as the man she had seen that afternoon.

As they sipped gin and tonic at a small cafe near the
Barrajas Plaza—"to make time while Alec showers and
changes," Esteban had told her—she said, "Tell me
about your cousin."

"What do you want to know?"

"How long has he been fighting?"

"For years. Let me see, he's thirty-three now, and he
started when he was fourteen. Nineteen years?"

"Is he popular?"

"God, yes!"

"But I've never heard of him. And I saw every fight
this spring."

"He's just come back from Mexico and South America. He's been on tour all winter."

"He's good, isn't he?"

"I think he's the best since Manolete or Arruza.
He'd be a multimillionaire if he hadn't had a run of bad
luck. But he's done all right. He has enough money
now to retire and live comfortably the rest of his life."

"What kind of bad luck?"

"He had a terrible *cornada,* a horn wound, the day
he made his debut here in Madrid. He was hooked in
the stomach, tossed and hooked again. When they
finally got the bull away from him, he managed to get to

his feet and walk to the *barrera*. I was sitting at ringside, too terrified to move. All I can remember hearing was the doctor screaming, 'Carry him! Carry him!' "

Esteban took a long sip of his drink. "They all said he wouldn't live through the surgery. But he did. Then two days later he got peritonitis and they said he wouldn't live through that. It took him a long time to recuperate, April. It was almost two years before he was strong enough to *torear*. Then it was like starting all over again."

She waited for him to go on.

"He's never been that badly hurt again, but he *has* been hurt. Every wound has taken its toll."

"Then why doesn't he quit?"

Esteban frowned at her over his glass. "Because he doesn't know anything else, I suppose. It's like your football or baseball players, April. What do they do when they're in their thirties? Alejandro has some good years left. He'll keep fighting as long as he can."

He glanced at his watch and signaled for the check. "It's almost eight. Things should be in full swing by now." When April hesitated he said, "Don't you want to meet him? Most women would give their teeth to be invited to one of his parties."

"Not this woman, *amigo*. I refuse to be a—a bullfight groupie. I'm only going to pick up my hat."

April could hear the music as soon as they stepped off the elevator on the fourteenth floor of the new apartment building on the Gran Vía: the slashing rhythm of the flamenco, the harsh Moorish wail of singers, the staccato click of heels.

"It's in full swing all right," Esteban said, taking her hand as he pushed open the apartment door.

Someone had rolled back an Oriental rug to the far end of the long living room, and a man and a woman were dancing, their faces serious, their bodies moving in perfect rhythm to the music of two guitarists. The people around them kept time, palm slapping against palm, as involved in the music as the dancers. Then, in a flurry of passion, the music rose to a frenetic pitch, faster and faster. Hard heels beat the floor. Faces tensed. Suddenly, breathlessly, in a burst of emotion that was almost palpable, the voices throbbed to a climax and it was finished.

"My God," April whispered, "I've never heard music like that."

"Fantastic!" Esteban said reverently. "Well, come on, let's try to find Alejandro."

It wasn't difficult. The matador sat in the middle of a large white sofa, a drink in his hand, completely surrounded by women.

He stood when he saw them, untangling himself from a gorgeous brunette who tried to cling to his arm.

He looked different, April thought as he came toward them; he looked even more attractive in the gray chinos and silver-gray velour shirt than he had looked that afternoon in his black suit of lights.

"Esteban!" He gripped his cousin's hand, then embraced him. "It's been too long, *mano*."

"Far too long. I heard you were back in Madrid but I've been in Jerez for two weeks. Just got back last night. I wouldn't have missed your *corrida* for anything in the world."

"Then I hope I gave you a good show." With a hint of a smile he turned to April and said, "And you, *señorita*? Did you enjoy the *corrida*?"

"Yes, I did, Señor Cervantes. But I seem to have lost something while I was there."

"Ah, the hat. But I hope you didn't worry. I hope you knew that I would guard it well."

He took her proffered hand and, looking closely at her, said, "I wondered what color your eyes were. And I told myself they must be green because of your red hair. But I was wrong, they're the color of cinnamon. An interesting combination."

April tugged her hand away as he said, "What may I fix you to drink, *señorita?* Whiskey? Wine?"

"Wine, please," she said as they moved toward the bar.

"White or red?"

"Red, please." She glanced at the wide stock of bottles behind the bar. "Château La Tour-Tigeac if you have it."

"Of course." His smile was amused. "Has my cousin been teaching you about wine?"

"Careful, *mano,*" Esteban warned. "Señorita Juneau probably knows more about wine than either of us. She comes from an old wine family in California. Alvarez took her away from them. He thinks she has the best wine-sniffing nose in the business next to Don José Ignacio Domecq."

"It's certainly a much prettier nose," Cervantes said as his eyes lingered on her face. "Juneau? That's French, isn't it?"

"Yes, my father came from Bordeaux," April said.

"And your mother?"

"Boston Irish."

"How long do you plan to be in Spain, *señorita?*"

"Another year perhaps."

"Then what? Will you return to your family in California?"

"No, *señor,* I'll go back to New York. I have an apartment there that I sublet before I left."

"Ah, yes. I forget that you American girls are not like our Spanish girls, who live at home with their parents until they marry. Our women, you see, are more protected than you Americans. It would never occur to them to live alone. Perhaps they're overprotected, inexperienced, but that is the way we Spaniards like our women."

"Is it really?" April's smile was pleasantly inquiring as she turned to look at the three girls still draped over the sofa, waiting for him to return, overpainted lips pursed to pouts, slinky skirts hiked up over rounded knees, as they shot angry glances her way.

As though to herself, she said, "Overprotected and innocent?" She bit her lip, not quite suppressing the giggle that spilled out. "One would hardly have guessed, Señor Cervantes."

His green Gypsy eyes flared with anger. Then, with that strange shadow of a smile, still not taking his gaze from hers, he said to Esteban, "We're almost out of the Manzanilla, *mano*. Would you mind getting a few more bottles from the kitchen?"

Without waiting for a reply, he took April's hand and said, "Señorita Juneau and I are going to collect her hat."

The hand that held hers was firm, and unless she wanted to make a scene, April had no choice but to follow him. She glanced once at the three girls on the sofa, smiling sweetly back when they glared at her.

Cervantes led her out to a balcony off the living room. In spite of her anger, she gasped as she saw the shimmer of lights stretched out below her, the sidewalk cafes along the Gran Vía and the sweeping play of colored lights from the fountain in the Plaza España.

Cervantes said, "You like Madrid?"

"I love it. I—I'll hate to leave."

"Then stay and marry Esteban. He's quite a catch."

"Esteban?" she said in genuine surprise. "We're just good friends. There's nothing romantic between us."

"I see." He captured her hand again and led her down the length of the balcony, slid open glass doors and pulled her inside a bedroom.

It was a large room and definitely a man's room. There were trophies of his profession there, including a pair of leather *zahones*—chaps—and a large poster, dated September 23, 1945, of a bullfight in Barcelona featuring Domingo Ortega, Manuel Rodriguez "Manolete" and Carlos Arruza.

"Who is the man in the drawing? Manolete?"

"No, Arruza. He fought a hundred and twelve *corridas* and four festivals that year. He suffered two *cornadas,* a serious one in Burgos the first of July and one in Manzanares in August. He was one hell of a *matador.*"

"Was?"

"He was killed in an auto accident near Mexico City. I'm sure that's not the way he would have chosen to die."

April knew, with a chill of certainty, that Alejandro meant it would have been better for the Mexican to have died in the bullring, but she didn't answer as she moved about the room, pausing before the bronze sculpture of a black bull and ornately carved silver spurs, and stopped to study an arrangement of photographs mounted over a mahogany desk: a younger Cervantes with Generalísimo Franco, one with Catherine Deneuve that looked fairly recent, another waterskiing with Princess Caroline of Monaco. Others with Roman Polanski, a chubby Christine Onassis . . .

April turned away from the photographs as Alejandro switched on the lamp at the bedside table.

Her pink hat lay in the middle of the dark fur spread that covered the king-size bed.

Glancing at him now she asked, "Why did you take it?"

"A whim. . . . Or perhaps I wanted to get you in my bedroom." His voice was mocking, and she felt that in some strange way he was making fun of her. He crooked a finger and said, "Come here, please."

"I will not! If you think for one moment that I'm going to—"

He looked at her with the same glint in his Gypsy eyes that he'd had that afternoon when he cited his bull for the kill. "You should wait until you're asked, Señorita Juneau. I only brought you in here to return your hat and to show you this painting."

He reached up and pulled a cord under the painting that hung over his bed.

"I thought you might like to see it. Now, please come over where you can see it properly."

She felt hot color creep to her cheeks and knew that she had no choice but to try to hide her embarrassment and show an interest in the painting.

"I bought it two days ago. No one has seen it except me. What do you think of it?"

The painting was of a woman, obviously Spanish, judging from her pale skin and dark eyes. She was seated on a straight-backed chair, the afternoon light slanting in through a narrow window, darkening the room as she strained to see the garment she was mending. On her head she wore a *pañoleta,* a small triangular scarf, and there was a dark shawl over her shoulders. The garment she was working on was a bullfighter's jacket. In her eyes there was a look of ineffable sadness.

To one side, near the window, was a small table. On

it was a picture of the Virgin and a small votive candle, its flame flickering in the twilight of the room.

"It's called *'Esposa del Matador'*—'The Bullfighter's Wife,'" Alejandro said. "What do you think of it?"

"It's beautiful." April moved closer, half kneeling on the bed as she studied the painting. "But I think I'd have to live with it awhile before I really understood it. Who is the artist?"

"Cossío del Pomar, a Peruvian. He lived in Spain for a long time. His sister was married to the great Spanish *matador* Juan Belmonte. I think perhaps he might have seen her, waiting like this, when Belmonte was in the ring. It's an interesting contrast to think about, isn't it? While her husband is performing before thousands of admiring fans, the sun on his face, filled with passion and excitement, she sits alone in the semidark, quietly mending his suit of lights."

"And praying for his safety," April said.

He took her hat from the center of the bed and handed it to her. "April is a funny name," he said.

"My parents didn't think so."

"It's a month, not a woman. April is springtime, rain and wild flowers. It's the promise of summer and—"

He reached out and touched her hair. "The promise of summer," he said again. "Well . . . perhaps."

And before she could stop him, he pulled her into his arms.

Chapter 2

HE STOPPED HER ANGRY PROTEST WITH HIS LIPS. HIS strong arms went around her back, forcing her tight against his body as his mouth demanded her response. When she tried to turn her head, his hands moved to her hair, his fingers spreading against her scalp as his mouth persisted, unrelenting and insistent, to force her lips apart. Then his tongue sought hers and his arms tightened around her.

Slowly, insidiously, her flame of anger turned to a small bright flame of desire. Not even aware that it was happening, April's lips softened and parted, returning his kiss because, for that brief moment she could not help herself.

When he left her lips to trail flaming kisses down the side of her neck to the hollow of her throat, her hands came up to press against his chest, pushing him away, and lingered against the softness of the silver-gray velour shirt—lingered to touch the spring of chest hair and the warmth of his skin. She barely managed to stifle a moan as his arms tightened and his lips once more crushed hers.

Then, as suddenly as he had taken her in his arms, he let her go. With the maddening flicker of a smile he said, "So what I have heard about red-haired *gringas* is true. You really do have fire in your veins."

April felt as though he had slapped her. Her nostrils flared in anger. "Latin men!" she managed to say. "You—you think all you have to do is grab a woman and she'll fall swooning in your arms."

As she said the words her anger grew. She hadn't swooned, but her response had been close enough. Now, because he mocked that response, she had to deny it. She faced him, cinnamon eyes blazing, and said, "That kind of treatment is . . . what one would expect from a savage, a caveman. It went out with seizing a lady by her hair and dragging her into a den. It's—"

Suddenly, April was flat on her back on the fur spread, arms pinioned on either side of her, looking up into the angriest eyes she had ever seen.

" 'A caveman, a savage'!" His voice shook with anger. "I will show you what *is* savage!"

His mouth covered hers, hard and hurting, forcing her lips apart, invading her mouth with his tongue, biting the corners of her lips when she tried to turn away.

Never, never, had she been kissed like that—so cruelly, so completely. It was as though he owned her, as though he could do—would do—anything he pleased with her. He kissed her until her lips felt bruised, until she felt as though her heart would leap from her body.

His lips moved to her throat but became gentle when he felt the panicked pulse of her heartbeat against his lips. He stopped then and raised his head to look at her. When he did, the anger went out of his green Gypsy eyes. He released her arms and kissed the tender inside of each captured wrist. Then he rolled on his side, pulling her close to him amid the lush softness of the fur, and his lips found hers again.

April's heart slowed to a flutter, and she felt her body soften against his as he kissed her slowly and deeply, running his tongue lightly over her passion-bruised lips. He trailed a soft line of fire down her throat and, with a breath, blew away the chiffon ruffle that hid her breasts.

"Please," she whispered, and felt the warmth of his lips against her skin. "Please," she said again, knowing that her voice trembled. Not sure whether it was from fear or need.

Cervantes let her go. When he looked down at her, his face was serious, puzzled. "I'm sorry," he said. "I don't usually behave this way. I've—I've never behaved this way before."

When she sat up, trying to smooth her hair into place, he pulled her hands away and ran his own over her shoulder-length silkiness. "It really is like fire," he murmured. "I've never seen hair that looked so alive." His hand paused against her face. "Will you have dinner with me tomorrow night?"

She shook her head.

"Please."

"No!"

He took her to Botin's.

The lovely rooms of the two-centuries-old restaurant near the Plaza Mayor had been furnished with taste and charm. As the maître d' led them down narrow spiral stairs, April saw that the low-ceilinged cellar had the atmosphere of another age. Even the waiters—elderly men, most of them—had an Old World charm.

When she picked up the menu, Alejandro Cervantes

said, "You're supposed to eat the roast suckling pig when you're at Botín's."

"I know—Hemingway. Would it be terribly gauche if I ordered steak instead?"

"Terribly." He motioned for the waiter. "Let's begin with *jamón serrano,* please. Then gazpacho. Then fresh asparagus and a green salad. Steak for the *señorita*— medium rare?—and I'll have the trout and a liter of sangria, please."

He hadn't asked her what she wanted, but instead of feeling resentful, April found herself leaning back against the cushions that lined the thick stone wall, feeling perfectly content and at ease as she relished the tantalizing odors and admired the quiet efficiency of the waiters and the ambience of the room.

She had not meant to have dinner with him, and even now she was not quite sure why she had agreed to it. Perhaps it was the two dozen red roses he'd sent her at the office that morning, roses that reminded her of flowers spilling on the sand of the bullring and of how truly magnificent he had been. Or perhaps it was because of the note that read:

> I'm abjectly sorry that I behaved like a barbarian.
> My only excuse is that, like the bulls yesterday, I
> was incited by the color red. Please let me make it
> up to you tonight at dinner.

In spite of herself, April had smiled, and when he phoned an hour later, she agreed to meet him that night.

"Alejandro Cervantes!" her secretary, Pepita, said when April put the phone down. "I didn't know you knew him."

"I met him last night."

"What's he like?" Pepita's wide dark eyes were alive with curiosity.

"Arrogant."

"Arrogant? Is that all you can say? Alejandro Cervantes is the handsomest, sexiest, most exciting man in Spain, and all you can say is that he's arrogant?"

April laughed. There was an easy friendship between her and Pepita that went far beyond a boss-secretary relationship. They lunched together often, went to movies together occasionally, and whenever it was possible, April took Pepita with her on business trips. A few weeks earlier Pepita had approached her to ask if April would consider taking her along as her secretary when she returned to New York, and April had conditionally said yes: provided she could clear it with Alvarez, she'd be delighted to have Pepita with her.

Now, thinking about Alejandro Cervantes, April said, "All right. I agree that he's rather good-looking."

"Rather good looking! *Dios mío!* The most sought-after man in Spain—no, not just in Spain: in Europe. Most women would do anything to go out with him." She hesitated, a frown marring her small piquant face. "But I forgot. You and Esteban—Señor Davalos, I mean—I forgot that he's your *novio,* your boyfriend. If you're serious about him . . ."

"But I'm not serious about him, and he's not my *novio,* Pepita. I'm very fond of him, but we're just friends. You went out with him a few times, didn't you?"

"A few times." The girl turned away from her for a moment, shuffling papers on her desk, then said, "What are you going to wear tonight? How about the dress you bought last week for the Domecq party?"

"Too formal." April's voice was purposely casual. "I'll find something. It's really not all that important to me."

But she left work early and went to a salon to have her hair washed and set in a new style, atop her head. The set was loose enough to look casual, with soft tendrils that curled around her face and the back of her neck. When it was time to get ready, she chose a dress of green silk that she had worn only once before.

It was a pale sea shade, form-fitting around her breasts and waist and flaring from hip to knee. With it she wore amber beads and earrings that added just the right touch of color and went well with her hair and eyes.

When Alejandro picked her up at nine, his glance swept over her, then returned to study her face. He reached out to touch a tendril curling over her ear and murmured to himself, "As I remembered."

They spoke little during dinner, but April was intensely aware of him—and curious. Although she enjoyed bullfights, she did not really know much about the art of *tauromaquia*, nor did she understand why a man would want to risk his life in a bullring.

As he poured sangria into their glasses, she asked, "Why do you fight, Alejandro?"

He set the pitcher carefully back on the table before answering, "Why do you breathe?"

"To live, of course!"

"That's why I fight."

April stared at him, shaking her head. "I'm sorry," she said, "I don't understand."

"I know." His voice was curiously gentle. "Few women do." He hesitated. "I was married. A long time ago, when I was twenty-three. It lasted less than a year."

"I'm sorry."

"Yes, so am I." He looked at her across the table, his face serious. "You see, she hated what I did. Well, not at first, I suppose. She married me, I think, because of who I was. And in the beginning she liked being a matador's wife. She liked the traveling, the excitement, the celebrity."

"What happened?"

"She fell in love with me."

"What?"

"She fell in love with me and her love made her afraid. Then it made her angry." He ran his long, tapering fingers along the half-full glass of sangria. "Perhaps if I'd been older, I might have understood how it was with her. But I was too full of myself then. I loved her, I suppose, but the bulls were my life. Maria ran a poor second."

"What happened to her?"

"She married an Italian film director we met in Cannes. We see each other every few years at some event or other. I think she's happy. I hope she is."

His green eyes searched her face. Then, as though making up his mind about something, he said, "I don't think I loved her as I should have, April, but perhaps I'm not able to love as completely as a woman needs to be loved. My profession is the most important thing in my life."

"I think I understand that it would demand total dedication, but surely human relationships and love are important too."

He shook his head and with a slight smile said, "Why do women get so deadly serious when they say the word *love?* Why can't they just relax and enjoy a relationship?"

"Before they move on to someone else?" April's voice was quiet.

"I didn't mean that. A man and woman can share a great deal. They can be friends as well as lovers, give to each other, care for each other."

"As long as it doesn't get . . . deadly serious?"

"That's right." His eyes were level. "And as long as they're totally honest with each other from the beginning."

There was a defiance in his look—and something else that she did not understand. She did not know why he would look at her as he did or why he had told her those things. She wanted to look away from those Gypsy eyes, wanted to say something, anything, to break the spell of his gaze.

But before she could speak, he took out his wallet and reached for the check. The moment he did so, the waiter appeared. As the man took the bills, he placed a bottle of cognac and two glasses on the table.

"Our best cognac, *Matador*," the waiter said with a smile.

"*Gracias, amigo*. The young lady and I will enjoy a taste after that excellent meal."

"A taste? As much as you like, *Matador*. With our compliments."

For a moment they sipped in silence, their eyes riveted upon each other. Then, tossing back the last of the cognac, he said, "Now, let's walk."

Outside, the night air was warm. The streets, as they always were at that time of night in Madrid, were crowded.

"You're not from Madrid?" she asked.

"No. I'm from Barcelona."

"I love that area," April said. "This weekend I'll be going up to Zaragoza. We have vineyards there."

Alejandro's face brightened.

"Then why not come up to Pamplona for the festival of San Fermín? It's only ninety miles. Have you ever been there?"

"No."

"If you're a Hemingway fan, you should go. Especially in July. The feria is from the sixth to the twentieth." He hesitated. "I'll be there for four *corridas,* April. I'd be happy to show you around."

She glanced at him. "I don't think so," she said.

"I'm sorry." He led her to one of the tables of a sidewalk cafe. After he had ordered two cappuccinos, he turned to her and said, "Why did you come out with me tonight?"

"Because I—I'm a pushover for red roses." She knew it was a flip answer, but it was the only one she could think of because she didn't know herself why she had come. The night before he'd been arrogant and rude. And yet . . . yet there was something about him that excited her. Perhaps it was the grace of his body, the proud way he held himself, the strength and sureness of his movements when he was in the bullring. He was an unusual man—and yes, she had to admit, the most physically attractive man she had ever met. In spite of his elegance, there was a certain wild Gypsy look about him that was perhaps due to his dark skin, his blue-black hair, and those wonderful green eyes.

She knew that he had been warning her at dinner, letting her know in a not-so-subtle way just exactly where she would stand if she became involved with him. But she had no intention of becoming involved with him.

When they finished their coffee they walked for a long time. Then they took a taxi to her apartment on Calle de la Magdalena. They were quiet in the taxi, but it was a comfortable silence. He held her hand, but he did not speak or attempt to kiss her.

When they reached her door, he unlocked it, then handed her the key and said, "If you change your mind about Pamplona, I'll be at the Hotel Los Tres Reyes."

"I won't change my mind," she said.

Alejandro put his hands on either side of the door so that she couldn't move away. He looked down at her, studying her face, his eyes curious. "I don't know what it is about you," he said. "You're beautiful, of course, but it's more than that. There's something so special . . . so wondrously feminine . . ."

He tried to smile that wry smile of his, but it didn't quite come off. "If I had any sense," he said, "I'd get as far away from you as I could. Because I have a feeling that I'd be safer facing a thousand-pound bull than I am looking into those wide brown eyes of yours." A muscle jumped in his cheek. "I could get lost in your eyes, *gringa*," he said softly, "and I don't want to get lost."

He kissed her then, a strange kiss that was both tender and passionate, a kiss that spoke of what already was and of what was to come. When Alejandro Cervantes released her, April knew that he had touched her in a way she had never been touched before.

Chapter 3

ZARAGOZA, ONCE THE SEAT OF THE ANCIENT KINGDOM OF Aragon, was a little over two hundred miles from Madrid. It was a drive April had made often during her past year in Spain, and she always enjoyed it, especially at times like this, with the hot summer sun turning the wheat to gold and the meadows into a riot of blossoming color.

When she arrived in Zaragoza she bypassed the city and drove to a small hotel on the other side of town, a homey place on the banks of the Río Ebro where she had stayed before.

She spent the night there and went to the vineyards the next morning. As always, there was the feeling of nostalgia for Napa Valley and her family when she saw the gold-green variegation of the terraced vineyards.

Wine, particularly Spanish wine, had been pleasing the world's palate for hundreds of years. Quantities of it were being shipped to England as early as the thirteenth century. April thought of *The Canterbury Tales* and of Chaucer, who no doubt spoke from

experience when he wrote, "This wine of Spaine cree-
peth subtilly."

Señor Fuentes, the plant manager, greeted her when
she drove in and took her immediately to the bodegas.

"Lovely," she said when she entered the huge cellar
with its great wooden casks, closing her eyes for a
moment to drink in the odor. "It reminds me of home."

"Then if your nose is happy, we will do some
sampling, *si?*" Señor Fuentes, a small elderly man with
red-veined cheeks and sky-blue eyes, smiled at her
affectionately. Using a long-handled dipper called a
venencia, he poured golden-colored sherry into a glass
and held it out to April.

She sniffed, then held the glass up to the light as she
studied the color. She took a sip, rolling it around on
her tongue before she swallowed.

It was superb—partly, she knew, because of something in the soil in that area of Spain that produced a
sherry unlike any other in the world. The *fino* that
April was tasting was a pale golden color, light and dry
and freshly fragrant with the delicate flavor of fresh
almonds.

"Perfect," she said with a smile.

"Ah." Señor Fuentes breathed a sigh of relief. "Now
an amontillado, eh?"

She sampled the sherries, made notes, and offered a
suggestion or two about plans for the year's harvest
festival before they went in to lunch, which consisted of
pot roast cooked in a spicy *chilindrón* sauce, red beans
and rice and a sinfully rich chocolate pastry. After
they'd eaten, April asked to see the vineyards, but
within an hour she had to beg off and return to the
hotel for a nap. The next day she went back to the
plant, did the work that needed being done and finished
inspecting the vineyards.

It was after three o'clock by the time she was through, too late to drive back to Madrid. She could return to the hotel or . . .

Her heart skipped three and a half beats. Or she could go to Pamplona to see the running of the bulls in the morning and the *corrida* in the afternoon.

April learned from Señor Fuentes that she did not have to return to Zaragoza to take the main road to Pamplona. She could continue on to Tudela and pick up the main highway there. He asked her if she had a hotel reservation and looked upset when she said no.

"But it is the feria," he said. "Rooms are hard to find."

"Oh, I'll get something," April said offhandedly, and ruefully chided herself for her dishonesty. She had lied to herself. She wasn't going just to see the running of the bulls and the *corrida;* she was going to see Alejandro Cervantes. She didn't know why, didn't even begin to understand this strange attraction. She only knew that when he put his arms around her, she felt something that she had never felt before.

She knew that it would be difficult to find a decent room in Pamplona. But she'd take anything, because it would only be for one night. She'd phone Alejandro tomorrow morning, perhaps meet him for the running of the bulls and return to Zaragoza after the *corrida*.

The *corrida*. She thought again of how he looked in the ring, of the strength and grace of his slim body, the way he held himself, the arrogance and pride of his movements. She felt herself shiver with a feeling that was half fear and half anticipation.

It was dark when she drove into Pamplona. The streets were crowded with people on this, the third day of the fiesta of San Fermín. April drove around and around the narrow streets of the main section of the town, trying desperately to find a place to park. When she finally spotted a car moving out, she positioned her small Spanish car to move in. She waited patiently while the car maneuvered out of the space, then noted with dismay that a Citroen, coming the wrong way on the one-way street, slowed, stopped and had the obvious intention of stealing *her* space.

"Damn!" she muttered under her breath, and blew her horn as the other car inched forward.

April held her breath as the car leaving the space moved out. Then, tightening her hands on the wheel, she shot around him and into the space, missing the Citroen by half an inch. She grinned triumphantly in spite of obscenities shouted at her in French and a gesture that she hadn't known was apparently universal until then.

But her triumph at finding a parking space was short-lived as she went from hotel to hotel, pension to pension, trying to find a room.

"You have no reservation?" The question was always the same. "Impossible, *señorita*. We begin taking reservations in August and September for next year's feria. Even the rooms in private homes are all taken. Believe me, unless someone has died, you will not find a room in Pamplona until after the feria."

All right, April thought, now what do I do? Sleep in my car? She cursed herself for being a fool, for trying to pretend she had come to see the running of the bulls. She had known from the moment Alejandro asked her to come that she would. But she had planned to phone him from the safety of her hotel room, to say in an offhand voice, "Hi, this is April Juneau. I decided this afternoon that it was a shame to be so close to Pamplona and not come." Perhaps he would have asked her to dinner. But now? If she phoned and said she had no place to stay, he would either think she was a fool or that she wanted to spend the night with him.

Finally, as hungry as she was tired, she found a restaurant on the Plaza del Castillo and, in spite of being upset, ate a grilled trout and a fresh green salad.

Half the people in the streets were drunk by the time April had finished her dinner and left the restaurant. She found it increasingly difficult to push by some of the men who not-so-good-naturedly tried to block her way.

At midnight she gave up and went to Los Tres Reyes. She had no choice, she told herself. She couldn't drive back to Zaragoza at that time of night, and she couldn't sleep in the car—not with so many drunks roaming the streets. It was ironic, she thought. She'd gotten herself into this dilemma because she wanted to see Alejandro Cervantes. Now she had to turn to him for help.

As April lifted her hand and knocked on Alejandro's door, she remembered the women who had surrounded him on the sofa the night she had met him. What if there was a woman with him now? What if . . . ?

She turned away just as the door opened. His blue-black hair was tousled. A white terry-cloth robe was knotted around his waist. When he ran a hand through his hair, April tried to look past him into the room.

"I—I'm sorry," she said. "It's late. I shouldn't have bothered you."

"You're not bothering me. Did you just arrive?"

"No, I got here three or four hours ago."

"But where have you been? What time is it anyway?" He took her arm and led her into a sitting room. "Good Lord," he said, glancing at a clock, "its midnight. What have you been doing?"

"Looking for a room." She was suddenly so tired, she thought she'd drop if she didn't sit down.

"You didn't make a reservation?"

April shook her head. "I know, I know. Dozens of people have already told me you can't come to Pamplona during the feria without a reservation. But I didn't plan to come." She looked up at him and bit her lip. "I don't know why I did."

"You came to see the running of the bulls." There was a slight smile on his lips.

"Yes."

"Have you had dinner?"

She nodded.

"You look exhausted. Where's your suitcase?"

"In the car."

"We'll get it tomorrow. I'll loan you a pair of pajamas for tonight."

"I can't stay here!"

"Of course you can. This is a suite, April. You can take the bedroom. I'll sleep here on the sofa."

"No, I couldn't possibly—"

"*Bueno.*" His grin was wicked. "If you insist, then we'll share the bed."

"I didn't mean—"

"Didn't you? Too bad. Now, come along." He took her hand and led her into the bedroom. He opened the suitcase on a bench near the window and handed her a pair of brown pajamas. "Clean towels in the bathroom," he said. "I'll wake you at six-thirty."

"Six-thirty!"

"You came to see the running of the bulls, didn't you?" Before she could answer, he put his arms around her and, tilting her face up to his, said, "Didn't you?"

Before she could answer, he kissed her, holding her

close so that she could feel the length of his muscular body against hers; kissed her thoroughly and completely. When he let her go, he said, in a voice that sounded as if he were out of breath, "Sleep well, April. I'll see you in the morning."

Burnished gold sparkled in the early-morning sun. April closed her eyes, then opened them and realized she was looking at the jacket of Alejandro's suit of lights. The suit he had worn a week earlier was black; this one was ivory. The jacket was embroidered with black braid, the epaulettes heavily encrusted with gold and silver. Beside it hung a vest and pants that she knew from Esteban were called breeches, or *taleguilla*.

She stared at the suit for a long time, wondering if Alejandro would fight that day, and wondering why she was there in Pamplona. She had told herself all that past week that she would not get involved with Alejandro Cervantes. He had made it quite clear the first and only time they had gone out how he felt about women. Only a fool would allow herself to care for a man who felt as he did. Yet, when he kissed her, when he drew her into his arms, it was as though she had no will of her own. She knew it would be easy—oh, so easy—to fall in love with him.

A light tap on the door interrupted her thoughts, and as she sat up, Alejandro came in carrying a tray and wearing the same white terry-cloth robe he'd worn the night before.

"Breakfast," he said, and when April smoothed the sheet and spread, he placed the tray across her lap and sat on the edge of the bed. "Did you sleep well?"

"Yes, thank you."

There were two cups on the tray, a pitcher of strong

black coffee, one of hot milk, a basket of assorted rolls, cheese and a jar of strawberry jam.

"No one ever brought me breakfast in bed before," she said without thinking.

"Oh? I'm surprised to hear that. I thought you American women . . ."

"Spare me!" April held her hand up in an angry protest. "I already know what you think of American women. Well, it's not true. We're not all as—as liberated or as promiscuous as you think."

"But surely you're not . . . ?" The word hung in the air.

"No, I'm not." Her angry eyes met his squarely. "I'm twenty-eight. I'm not an angel. But neither am I promiscuous. There was a man. *One man.* We lived together for six months."

"What happened? Ah, you came to Spain and left him behind. That's it, isn't it?"

"No, Señor Cervantes. That is not it. He left me."

"But why?"

Suddenly the memories were back. Memories of Ross. Of that last night when he'd packed his clothes, folding them with excruciating neatness while she watched from the door. He'd said, in that maddeningly reasonable voice of his, "But we knew it wasn't permanent when we moved in together, April. I didn't promise forever. It's been marvelous and now it's over. Let's not have a scene."

"There's someone else!"

"Of course there's someone else. Hand me my shaving cream, will you, dear?"

She hadn't handed him the shaving cream; she'd thrown it at him—and had thrown everything else of his she could put her hands on, hooting with derision when he grabbed his half-packed, not-so-neat-after-all suit-case and headed for the door.

Now, as she looked at Alejandro, she said, "One man. No one before or since," and wondered why it was important that he know that.

"Are you still in love with him?"

"God, no!"

"Then drink your coffee."

April looked at him. She didn't understand him. One moment he was arrogantly macho, the next almost touchingly kind. She was glad that she'd told him about Ross and thankful for the understanding she saw in his face.

"The *encierro*, the running of the bulls, starts at eight o'clock," he told her. She knew then that the subject of Ross was closed. "People have been finding places on the street since before sunup."

"Is that where we'll be? On the street?" She wasn't sure how close she wanted to be to a bunch of stampeding bulls.

Alejandro shook his head, taking a bite of his roll. "My manager's hotel is near the city hall. We'll watch from there. Finish the rolls, April. We won't have dinner until after the *corrida*."

"What about lunch?"

He shook his head. "I'm fighting today. Matadors never eat before a fight."

She felt the nervous jump of her heart in the sudden stillness of the room. She put the roll back on her plate and said, "Really? Why?"

"Because if there's an accident, the surgeon will have less difficulty."

"I see." She felt as if there were not enough air in the room.

He spread some of strawberry jam on her roll and handed it to her. She took a bite and found that it was difficult to swallow.

"I'm not very hungry," she said apologetically. "I guess because I had dinner so late last night."

"All right. We'll get you a snack later." He moved the tray off her lap. "The shower is yours whenever you want it."

"Thank you."

When she got out of bed, the legs of the pajamas dragged on the floor and the arms hung three inches below her fingertips.

"You look like a refugee," Alejandro said with a smile.

April smiled back, pushing the sleeves up, then tried to brush the long auburn hair back from her face, looking at him uncertainly as he moved toward her.

"Alejandro . . . Alejandro, I . . ."

"You've got a smear of jam on your face," he said, and bent to kiss it away from the corner of her mouth. Then his lips were against hers in a warm, searching strawberry kiss as his arms gathered her close.

April felt herself sway against him, lost in the warmth of his mouth, the tender explorations of his tongue, the feel of his lean body against hers. So caught up was she in the stirring closeness of him that she was almost unaware that his hands had slipped under the pajama top to caress her back.

He raised his mouth from hers for the breath of a moment and looked down at her with his green Gypsy eyes, eyes that held the heat of his passion as he whispered her name before he bent again to seek her mouth.

When his hands moved around her back to find her breasts, she could not stop her small involuntary gasp of pleasure. She wanted to pull away—knew she had to pull away. But oh, the feel of his hands, the warmth and magic of them, the delicate touch of his fingers caressing her nipples.

April melted with desire. Never had she wanted a man as much as she wanted this one. But she couldn't. She couldn't. Oh, Lord, if only he would stop so she could think. If only he would not touch her this way.

With a deep, shuddering breath she pulled away from him. "No," she said. "No."

"But why?" His eyes looked glazed with desire. "Why, April? You don't want to stop any more than I do. You want me as much as I want you."

"Alejandro, please."

"No!" His hands tightened on her shoulders. "Tell me why."

"Because we're different. We want different things. Because you—you have other women. A lot of them, from what I saw the other night at your apartment. And I can't . . . I won't ever be a part of a group."

"And you think that's all you mean to me? Just another woman I'm adding to my collection?"

"Yes." She put her hands on his shoulders and looked up at him, her eyes serious. "You don't even know me, Alejandro. I'm just another redhead to you. Another—"

"Another redhead! In Spain?" She saw the corners of his mouth twitch in a smile. Then with a sigh he said, "All right, *gringa*. I won't bother you again. At least not this morning. I don't know why I bothered anyway; with those brown pajamas on you look like an undernourished boy."

"An undernourished boy! You really are a bas—"

But before she could finish the word, he'd pulled her back into his arms, and with his lips moving insistently on hers, his hands slipped inside the back of her pajama pants and cupped her buttocks, forcing her closer to him. He held her like that while his lips and his tongue devoured her mouth; held her until she was weak with longing.

Then abruptly he took his mouth from hers. And before she could move away, he gave her a sharp smack against her bare skin and said, "Now, go take that shower."

Chapter 4

THE BARRICADED STREETS WERE A CRUSH OF PEOPLE, SOME looking fresh and clean from at least part of a night's sleep, others bleary-eyed, obviously barely recovered from the previous night's wine even as they started this day's bacchanalia. Boys from Harvard, Oxford and Heidelberg; girls from Bryn Mawr, UCLA and the Sorbonne tumbled, rumpled and worn, from cars and park benches where they had slept for two or three hours.

The early risers squinted in the sunshine, sniffed the aroma of fresh hot rolls drifting from the town's bakeries and came awake finally with the beat of drums and the blare of trumpets as a marching band rounded the corner of the square.

Most of the men who would run that day were dressed in white shirts and pants, with red sashes around their waists and red scarves around their necks. Those who didn't have white shirts and pants at least had red scarves to signal they would be among the runners.

Alejandro, dressed in jeans and a blue and white checked shirt, steered April through the throng of people, who were pushing their way along the narrow streets or jockeying for positions behind the barricades. Young boys fought each other to climb lamp posts; others perched on building ledges or crouched in niches. Every available balcony overflowed.

"I've never seen so many people out so early," April said, clutching Alejandro's arm as he maneuvered her through the crowd.

"There are probably two hundred thousand tourists in Pamplona this week."

"Two hundred thousand!" She dodged a group of boys barreling down the street toward the square. "Where do the bulls come from? How do they get here?"

"They're brought across the river at midnight and put into a temporary corral at the bottom of Santo Domingo Street. When they're released, they'll run from Santo Domingo on up to the town hall and along the streets, then through an open square that takes them into the bullring. The course is a little over nine hundred yards and they cover it in about two and a half minutes."

"That fast?"

"A bull is fast, April. Faster than a racehorse over a short distance." He stopped in front of a small hotel, leading her inside and up to a room on the second floor. "It's Alec," he called when he knocked.

"Where the hell have you been?" a man in his mid-sixties asked as he opened the door. "It's almost eight. Another few minutes and the *encierro*—" He stopped and stared at April before his gaze swung back to Alejandro. "Sorry," he apologized. "I didn't realize you had company."

"April, this is my manager, Carlos Manzanares. Carlos, the Señorita April Juneau."

"Juneau? You are French?" The man who asked the question was tall and distinguished-looking. His skin was fair, but his eyes, looking at her now with a hint of disapproval, were a dark, penetrating brown.

"No, *señor*," April said in her excellent Spanish. "I'm an American."

"But your Spanish is very good." Then, remembering his manners, he opened the door wider and ushered them into the room. "It's five minutes to eight," he said. "We will hear the first *aviso* soon. Is this your first visit to Pamplona, Señorita Juneau?"

"Yes. I can't believe how many people are here."

"Too many. It's impossible to find a room." He hesitated. "You were able to find something, *señorita?*"

"I got April a room at Los Tres Reyes," Alejandro interjected before she could answer. "She got in quite late last night."

A frown creased Manzanares's forehead. "I hope you got some rest, Alec."

But before Alejandro could respond, an explosion split the air. He took April's arm and, leading her out to the balcony, said, "That's the first signal. It means the bulls have been freed from the pen and have started their run. A second rocket will go off when all the bulls are on their way."

Below them they saw the excited movement of the crowd. The white-shirted men with their red sashes and scarves waited for their first glimpse of the animals.

Then there was another explosion and another rocket whistling through the clear morning air, and suddenly there they were: the bulls, horns gleaming in the sun, hooves beating against the pavement.

The men below, tense now, turned to run, shoving

one another, shouting in their excitement. They ran with great bursts of speed, the bulls close on their heels. But the bulls were fast, and it was difficult to keep ahead of them, especially in the crush of so many men. When the beasts caught up with the runners, the more agile spun to one side, their bodies flat against the buildings, clawing for a foothold as they tried to climb up, away from the horns.

One man fell. The man behind him fell over him. Someone shouted a warning. Another man fell. And another. And suddenly there was a scrambled pileup of shouting, cursing, grunting men, the bellow of animals and the sound of hooves striking flesh and bones.

"They'll be killed!" April cried, staring down in horror at the men.

"A few cuts and bruises," Alejandro said. "The bulls won't stop to attack once they've started running. It's only when an animal gets away from the herd that he panics."

"Why in the world would anybody want to do that?" she said, gasping as one of the bulls struck a man in the back with his snout, knocking him against a building. The man cried out in fear as he tried to climb out of reach of the saber horns. April screamed as a boy of eighteen or nineteen faced an oncoming bull, trying to *torear* with a folded-up newspaper.

Beside her Alejandro sucked in his breath and said, "Christ!" only a second before one of the animal's horns caught the boy under his armpit, threw him up, then slammed him to the ground. As the horns reached for him again several of the onlookers reached under the barricades and pulled the boy to safety.

As suddenly as it had begun, it was over. The bulls were past them, running down the street toward the bullring, where other fans waited. Below them the people began to disperse. In the distance April could hear the wail of an ambulance siren.

"Come and have some coffee," Señor Manzanares said. "You look a bit pale, Señorita Juneau. Was this all a bit too much for you?"

It was the tone of his voice more than the words. A taunting tone that seemed to say, "Well, you're an American. What can one expect?"

"It wasn't too much for me, Señor Manzanares. It's just that I'm always a bit put off at how some men feel they must prove their virility."

"Touché!" Alejandro said with a laugh, a laugh that his manager did not join in with.

The conversation was polite but forced while they drank their coffee. April sat back, letting the men do most of the talking.

Carlos Manzanares, she discovered, had been Alejandro's manager for almost twenty years. He was bossy the way a father is bossy—not in a superior or an unkind way, but as one who is older and sure that he knows what is best.

Alejandro listened to him, nodding in agreement as the older man told him that after the four fights in Pamplona they would go to Valladolid. "You'll fight in Barcelona on the twentieth," Manzanares said. "Valencia on the twenty-seventh." Then, with a glance at April, he asked, "What about the *sorteo* today? Do you want to go or shall I take care of it?"

"I'll go with you, Carlos." Then, turning to April, he said, "The *sorteo* is the drawing for the bulls we'll fight this afternoon. They're paired, the best three with the remaining three, so the division will be fair. A bull with small horns will be paired with one with large horns, for example. And once they're paired, the name and numbers are written down, rolled into a ball and thrown into a hat. Either the matadors or their managers choose a ball.''

When they left Manzanares, Alejandro suggested they find her car and get her suitcase so that she could go back to Los Tres Reyes and change. But April couldn't remember where she had parked the car, and by the time they found it, it was time for the *sorteo*. He hurried her back to the room, kissed her briefly and told her he'd be back in an hour or two.

After April unpacked the outfit she planned to wear to the *corrida,* she settled down on the sofa with a paperback and read until she began to feel drowsy. Just before she drifted off to sleep, she thought about Carlos Manzanares and his obvious displeasure that she was there. She was still worrying about it when she awoke an hour later. She lay for a few minutes, arms above her head, gazing up at the ceiling and wondering what she was doing there in Alejandro Cervantes's suite. Was she, God forbid, about to turn into a bullfight groupie?

But that wasn't why she was there and she knew it. She had known from the very first time that Alejandro Cervantes had kissed her that something important had happened between them. She didn't think she was ready for it and she knew she didn't want it. If she had any sense, she'd be halfway back to Madrid at that moment.

But running away wouldn't help. She just had to be sure she was going into this with her eyes open and thinking straight. She'd been hurt once by a man who didn't want to make a commitment, and she had no intention of allowing that to happen ever again.

It wasn't that she criticized women who went from one man to another, telling themselves each time that "This is it." A year with one man, six months with another, two years, two weeks, and by the time they were thirty, they'd lived with a dozen men. It just wasn't the kind of life she chose to live.

Alejandro Cervantes was a dangerously attractive man in a profession that gave him an irresistible flare of glamour. Even without that aura April knew that he would be an easy man to care for, an easy man to fall in love with.

But April had no intention of falling in love with him.

After she showered she dressed in a pair of royal-blue suede knickers, a matching suede jacket and a white silk ruffled blouse. She was just fastening gold earrings in her ears when Alejandro came in.

He smiled when he saw her. "You look like a Gypsy," he said.

"So do you."

"Ah, but I have a reason to. My grandmother is a Gypsy."

"Really?"

He nodded. "My grandfather went to Seville when he was twenty and he met my grandmother there. She was sixteen." He cocked one black brow. "The story is that he kidnapped her."

"Kidnapped her?" April laughed. "How exciting!"

"It was the only way he could get her away from her family. Her brothers followed them and tried to kill Granddad, but he got away and took my grandmother to Granada, where he found a priest to marry them. When they finally got back to Barcelona six months later, the family was furious because he'd married a Gypsy, but by that time grandmother was pregnant and there wasn't anything they could do. They had eleven children and a lot of good years together before my grandfather died. My grandmother is still living; I want you to meet her, April. I think you'd like her."

"Does she live in Barcelona?"

"Yes, but she spends a lot of time at my ranch." He hesitated. "Did you find room to hang your clothes?"

"I didn't unpack."

Alejandro's dark brows rose in question.

"I'm going to Zaragoza as soon as the *corrida* is over."

"Why not stay one more day?"

"I don't think so."

"April, I—" He took a step toward her just as someone knocked on the door. With a frown he said, "That's Paco. He's come to help me dress."

When the man came in, he shook April's hand and seemed not at all surprised to find a woman in the suite. Alejandro sent down for coffee for them and a sandwich for April. When the waiter brought the order, Alejandro and Paco went into the bedroom.

And when Alejandro came out, it seemed to April that he was a totally different man, a stranger from an earlier age.

The ivory gold-encrusted jacket and vest, the pants with the trim on the sides, were all skintight. The pink thigh-length stockings with the embroidered arrow decoration on the side fitted snugly under the pants. He wore a starched white ruffled shirt under the jacket, and a narrow red tie. His feet were clad in heelless black leather slippers, and in his hand he carried his *montera*, the black hat. When he turned to say something to Paco, April saw the *coleta*, the small black pigtail, fastened to the back of his hair.

He looked at her, his eyes serious and intent.

Paco said, "I will wait in the hall, *Matador*."

Alejandro nodded. When they were alone, he handed a ticket to April and said, "I'm sorry you'll have to sit alone, but both Paco and Carlos will be in the *callejón* with me. I will see you back here as soon as it's over and we'll go to dinner."

"I thought I'd leave directly from the bullfight, Alejandro."

"That's impossible. You can't take your suitcase to the plaza."

"No, but I could put it in the car before I go."

"Don't be silly, April. If you insist on leaving, I'll take you to your car later."

"Alejandro, I—"

"I haven't time to argue with you. Just be here when I return." Then, perhaps because he realized that what he had just said sounded like an order, he added, "April, please. I want to see you before you go."

He put his hands on her shoulders and drew her to him. She could feel the roughness of the gold-encrusted epaulettes against the thinness of her blouse. She knew when he kissed her that the reason she wanted to leave was because she was afraid. Afraid she might get lost in his arms.

His first bull had small horns and weak legs. Alejandro fought it as well as he could and dispatched it without fanfare. The next matador had better luck with his bull. But the third animal followed the matador's cape right into the fence, snapped off a horn, and had to be taken out of the ring with the help of the oxen. The substitute bull was worse than Alejandro's had been, and by the time it received the coup de grâce, the crowd was in an ugly mood.

I hope the next bull is better, April thought. The crowd was angry and she didn't want Alejandro to suffer their wrath. From her seat in the first row, right in front of the *burladero de matadores,* where the matadors all stood, she saw Alejandro glance at the door through which the next bull would enter the ring.

The door was flung open and the bull exploded into the plaza. Big and black, with a wide set of perfect horns, he hesitated only a moment. Then with a bellow of rage he raced toward Alejandro.

"Ahaaa, toro!" Alejandro called, holding the magenta and yellow cape in front of him. *"Ahaaa!"*

The bull, head down, horns thrust forward, charged the cape as Alejandro executed a perfect *verónica,* passing the bull to one side. Then, having bent the line of the charge, Alejandro lowered his cape and, with a graceful movement of his arms, brought the animal back past his body.

He did *verónica* after *verónica,* finishing the series with a beautifully slow *remate* that brought the crowd to its feet with shouts of *"Olé! Olé, Matador!"*

When the *picadors* entered the ring on their padded, blindfolded horses, the non-Latins, not realizing the necessity of slowing the animal down so that he could be played, began to whistle. Alejandro allowed only one pic and did three lances, and the *picadors* left. Then came the *banderilleros* to plant the sticks, and finally it was time for the final act of the drama.

When Paco handed Alejandro his sword and *muleta,* the red cape, Alejandro came to stand before April.

The man next to her said, "You must stand, Señorita."

Heads turned. There were excited whispers.

"This is for you, *gringa,*" Alejandro said. Then, turning his back, he tossed the *montera* over his shoulder.

"Gracias, Matador," April said as she caught the hat. *"Muchas gracias."*

Alejandro began the *faena* close to the fence, citing the bull for an *ayudado por alto,* remaining still as he provoked the charge; then, without moving his feet, he turned his hands slightly out away from his body, swaying the cloth as the bull thundered by.

He followed this with a series of *naturales,* then an *afarolado,* passing the bull by moving the *muleta* to the side and whirling it over his head as the horns brushed by his body. Then a series of passes that were so daring, they made April want to cover her eyes, for as he called the bull to him he deliberately looked away from it into the crowd, again and again, completely immobile as the bull brushed his body.

The crowd exploded with shouts of *"Olé!"* and *"Torero, Torero!"* and the band played *dianas,* the traditional music that cheers a matador on.

It was almost time for the kill when he tried a low *trincherazo.* His feet were firmly planted as he brought the bull past him with a smooth movement of the waist and wrist.

But no—not past!

The bull slowed. Jerked his great head. Slashed out.

One stiletto-sharp horn caught Alejandro's leg, caught him, lifted him and slammed him to the sand.

April jumped from her seat, hand to her mouth to stop the rising scream.

His *cuadrilla* rushed into the ring to call the bull away from him. But when Paco tried to help him, Alejandro pushed the man away and leaped to his feet. Then, obviously trying not to limp, he allowed himself to be led to the fence. Blood ran down his calf.

"He's all right," the man beside her said. "It's just a leg wound."

Just a leg wound! April wanted to hit him.

Quickly, Carlos and Paco wrapped a bandage around

the blood-soaked stocking. Then Alejandro, his face showing his anger and impatience, motioned them away and turned back to the ring as shouts of approval rang through the plaza.

Quietly, calmly, moving as though nothing had happened, Alejandro called the bull to him. He made a series of dramatically emotional passes, completely ignoring the blood that seeped through the bandage, down his leg and onto the sand. But his face was white, his brows drawn together in a grimace of pain by the time he cited for the kill.

When it was finished and he was awarded two ears, he limped to the center of the ring and, instead of making a triumphant tour, simply raised his arms to the crowd, then walked slowly back to the fence. With Paco on one side of him and Carlos on the other, he disappeared down the *callejón*.

April sat as though she'd been frozen to her seat as another bull ran into the ring and another matador rushed out to fight him.

She felt helpless, paralyzed by fear, not sure what she should do, wondering whether or not she should try to find the infirmary and if she would be allowed to see Alejandro if she did find it. Or would they take him to a hospital?

She had to move, had to do something, because she could not sit there another minute wondering what was happening to him. She jumped up from her seat and started to make her way out of the plaza when she saw Paco coming toward her.

"The *matador* says for you to go back to the hotel and wait for him there," he said before April could speak.

"How is he?"

"The wound is deep, but he will be all right. The

doctor is attending him now." He took her arm, and his nice face wrinkled in concern as he said, "Are you all right, *señorita?* You look worse than Alejandro."

"I'm fine," April managed to say.

"And you will wait for him at the hotel?"

She hesitated for a fraction of a second, then nodded and said, "Yes. Yes of course I'll wait for him."

Chapter 5

"YOU DIDN'T LEAVE," ALEJANDRO SAID WHEN HE SAW her.

"No." April tried not to show how worried she was. "How . . . how is your leg?"

"Painful," Manzanares snapped before Alejandro could answer. "We've got to get him to bed."

"I found clean pajamas and put them out."

"Thank you. We'll take care of him now. I'll stay tonight in case he needs anything."

There was no doubt, from either his tone or his words, that he had dismissed her. But before April could reply, Alejandro broke in. "That's kind of you, Carlos, but if you'll just help me out of my clothes, I'll be able to manage. And since Señorita Juneau is in the same hotel, I'm sure she wouldn't mind looking in on me tonight."

His voice, in spite of the obvious pain he was in, was firm. And so Carlos, his face stiff with barely suppressed anger, nodded to Paco, and together the two men helped Alejandro into the bedroom. When they had him in bed, Carlos came to tell her that there were two bottles of pills and that Alejandro was to take two of each of them every four hours. "He's had penicillin and a tetanus shot," he said, "but nothing for the pain. He didn't want anything that might make him sleep until he got back here." His voice dripped with his disapproval, and with a severe purse of his lips he said, "Call me immediately if you think he's worse."

"Of course."

Still, Manzanares hesitated, his hand on the door. "Alejandro is a stubborn man. He won't tell you if he is in pain or if he feels worse. You have to look beyond his words to see. . . ." He shook his head. "It's difficult to explain."

"I'll watch him. Please don't worry."

By the time April went back into the bedroom, Alejandro was groggy. He reached for her hand and, with a slight grin, said, "I'm sorry. I know I trapped you. But I didn't want you to leave."

She squeezed his hand. "And I didn't want to go until I was sure you were all right. Is the pain better now?"

"Yes."

"I was terribly frightened."

"These things happen, April." His eyes closed and he yawned. "Damned pills," he mumbled.

"Go to sleep. I'll be here."

"You don't mind the sofa?"

"Of course not. Go to sleep, Alejandro."

But April didn't sleep on the sofa that night. Instead, when she had changed to her gown and robe, she curled up in a chair near the bed so that she could watch him. In four hours she awoke him and gave him the pills. He swallowed them and immediately went back to sleep.

When she was sure that he was comfortable, April set the alarm, then settled down in the chair for a nap. When she gave him his next dosage of pills, he asked what time it was, and when he saw the light beside the chair, he said, "You don't have to sit up with me, April. Go to bed."

"I want to be where I can see you."

He caught her hand. "Then come to bed with me."

"Alejandro!"

"You'll be safe. I'm so groggy I can't even lift my head." He gave her hand a tug. "I promise on my grandmother's good name that I—" He winced in pain.

"Lie down." April eased him back against the pillow. "The pills will help in a minute. Close your eyes. That's it. Easy now." She brushed the hair back from his face and, in a voice that was barely above a whisper, said, "Sleep now, Alec. Sleep."

When the doctor arrived at eight-thirty the next morning, April touched Alejandro lightly on his shoulder and whispered, "The doctor is here." Then she went to the door.

Dr. Enfante was a portly, gray-haired man with sideburns, a large wilted mustache and a nice smile. He examined Alejandro's leg, gave him another injection of penicillin and said, "The leg's coming along, *Matador*. There's no sign of infection."

And to April he said, "Keep him in bed today. No shower; just give him a sponge bath."

She glanced at Alejandro and saw his maddeningly innocent smile. When the doctor left, he put his hands behind his head and said, "I'll have my bath now if it's not too much trouble."

Hands on her hips, April looked at him. Then, with a slight smile, she said, "I have a feeling you're better."

She went into the bathroom and came back with a soapy washcloth and a towel. "Wash your face," she ordered in a no-nonsense voice. "I'll do your back and chest."

He nodded, grinning at her as he slipped out of the top of his pajamas.

April had never bathed a man before. She found it a strange but not unpleasant experience. Alejandro's body was firm and muscular—not with the bulging, overdeveloped muscles of a man who lifts weights, but with the firm, smooth muscles of a fine athlete. For just a moment she had an almost irresistible desire to run her fingers over his smooth bronze skin and the patch of curly black chest hair that ran to a thin line and disappeared under his pajama bottoms.

She looked away. "I—I'll do your legs now," she said as she lifted the blanket back and rolled up one pajama leg, noting that his legs were as perfect as the rest of him, long and lean, well shaped, the muscles like steel. April washed around the bandage carefully, then rinsed away the soap and wiped his legs dry.

When she stood up, Alejandro's eyes widened innocently and he said, "You mean you've finished?"

April bit her lip and marched into the bathroom to rinse the washcloth. When she came back she handed it and the towel to him and said, hoping she sounded impersonal, "You can do the rest while I get fresh pajamas and phone down for breakfast."

"*Muy bien, señorita.* And *gracias.* You give a wonderful, if incomplete, bath."

He slept most of the day. When he awoke he stretched and said, "I've been dreaming about a Basque village that I haven't seen in years. Pasajes de . . . ? Damn, what was it? Pasajes de . . . San

Pedro. Yes, that's it. It's a few miles from San Sebastián, near the French border. Have you ever heard of it?"

April shook her head.

"Not many people have, I guess." He reached out and took her hand. "I dreamed that you and I were there together."

"Alejandro . . ."

"Let's go, April. Let's go to Pasajes."

"I can't."

"Why not?"

"I—I have to go back to work."

"Can't you phone and ask for a few days off?"

"I've got some vacation time coming, but I—I can't go away with you."

"We could lie on the beach all day," he said. "Swim and walk and talk and . . . and eat broiled sardines." His hand tightened on hers. "Come to Pasajes with me, April."

Slowly she shook her head. "I'm sorry, Alejandro. But I can't do that."

She turned away before she could change her mind. She ordered sandwiches from room service, then, after they had eaten, gave him his pills and, in a coolly brisk voice, said, "These will help you sleep. If you need anything, just call me. I'll leave the door to the sitting room open."

Alejandro nodded. "I appreciate everything you've done, April. Thank you."

"There's no need for thanks." Her voice was stiff.

She was trembling as she undressed in the other room, hating herself for having been so cool and unloving. But Alejandro had asked her to make a bigger step than she was prepared to make, because she knew that once she crossed that line with him, she would never be able to go back. She bit her lip, wanting to rush to him now, to tell him that yes, she would go with him to Pasajes or any other place he wanted to go.

With shaking fingers she switched off the light and lay down on the sofa, closing her eyes, willing herself to relax.

Alejandro winced when he saw her light go off. He knew he'd been a fool to ask her to go away with him, a fool to think she might want to.

He did not think he had ever felt quite that way about a woman before. It was not just because she was beautiful. She was, of course, but it was more than that. There was an essence about her, a spirit and a promise that seemed lacking in other women, a warmth and tenderness that touched something in him that was almost as overwhelming as the physical attraction he felt. And God knew he felt that and had from the first time he'd laid eyes on her.

He remembered that first night in his bedroom in Madrid. Even then, with dozens of guests waiting, he'd wanted to throw April down on the bed and make love to her until she was breathless with passion, until she whispered his name and told him she wanted him as much as he wanted her. God, how he wanted to hear her whisper her need against his lips.

April, he thought with something like desperation. April. . . . And finally he slept.

To dream of the bulls.

To dream that he was young again and that his legs were strong.

He stood in the center of a bullring, and the band played a *paso-doble* as he looked toward the gate through which his bull would emerge.

But something was strange. There was more than one gate. One in front of him, one to his left, one to his right. One behind him.

"No!" he protested. "This isn't the way it's done."

But before anyone could hear his protest, all four gates opened and all four bulls rushed into the ring.

He could move only in slow motion, the *capote* held in front of him, more as a shield than a lure. With his heart beating like a sledgehammer, he faced the bull that came from directly ahead, passed him, then whirled to face the next bull. The next and the next.

The animals wheeled for another charge and lowered their heads to rush him.

I can't do this, his mind screamed. It isn't fair. I can't fight them all.

"No!" he shouted. "No!" as the biggest of them all lowered his great head.

Alejandro took a step backward on his leaden feet. He could feel the bull's breath on his face, smell the animal smell, see the small bloodshot eyes.

The bull lunged. Alejandro cried out again, then fell and tried to roll away as horns reached for his body. He cried out, "Oh, Jesus! Jesus!"

"Alejandro! Alejandro!"

"No!" he shouted. He grabbed April's arms and shook her. "No!"

"Shhh. Wake up, Alec. Wake up."

His eyes focused on her face. Then with a groan he pulled her to him and rested his head against her breasts, trying to block out the dream, hanging on to her, holding her as though he would never let her go.

April held him like that for a long time before she gently eased him down in bed. But his hands reached for her, and in a voice that shook with need, he said, "No, don't leave me."

She looked at him for a long moment, then with a small sigh pulled back the sheet and lay down beside him, pulling him into her arms, his head in the hollow of her shoulder as she stroked his hair. Finally the trembling stopped and he slept.

The bands woke her at dawn. She and Alejandro had shifted positions in the night, and now she lay close to his chest and his arms were around her. I have to get up, she thought. I have to . . . and drifted back to sleep.

The late-morning sun streaming in through the window awoke her. She lay for a few moments, feeling the warmth of the man who slept next to her; then, edging slightly away, she studied his face: the thick black hair, tousled now; the long black lashes, which lay like shadows against his cheeks; the slim, straight nose; the sensuously curved lips.

He moved in his sleep, his hand twitching nervously on her waist, his black brows drawn together in a frown.

What kind of dreams bedeviled him? she wondered, remembering how he'd clung to her the night before, his body wet with perspiration and terror. How vulnerable, how different, he'd been from the confident man who strode into the bullring to face and dominate a giant of a bull. It was the bulls he dreamed of, she thought with a sigh. The bulls, which possessed both his waking and sleeping hours.

And as she studied his face, he opened his eyes and said, "I had a dream."

"I know."

He rubbed a hand through his hair. "A nightmare. I'm sorry."

"It's all right. How do you feel?"

"Better. The leg doesn't hurt."

"That's good." It suddenly struck her as odd that it didn't *seem* odd that she should be lying in bed, talking to this man she barely knew. And because she knew she shouldn't have been there, she eased away and said, "Are you hungry?"

"Starving." His eyes warmed as he studied her face.

"Well . . . that's a good sign. I'll—I'll phone down for breakfast."

"But I don't want food."

"Alejandro . . ."

His arms tightened around her, pulling her back close to him.

"Let me up," April protested, hoping she sounded firm, trying to ignore the warmth she felt with his body so close to hers and the feel of his hand caressing her back. "Let me up," she said again.

"In a minute." He tilted her face to his.

"We shouldn't—" April began, even as his mouth covered hers. "We—" as her lips parted and she shivered with pleasure.

Then his hands, his slim, elegant hands, began to stroke the length of her, touching, caressing, learning the lines of her body, finally moving slowly to touch her breasts.

"No," April whispered, her lips against his throat. "No," as her body moved toward his.

"I think yes," Alejandro murmured, searching for her mouth again. "Yes and yes and yes."

April closed her eyes, allowing herself to relax, to be carried away on a cloud of sensation as his hands cupped the fullness of her breasts and his fingers made torturous circles that came closer and closer to the peaked tips. When at last he touched them, it was with such infinite tenderness that April felt all of her restraint, all of her defenses, melt away.

"Alec," she said. "Oh, Alec."

He kissed the corners of her mouth and the side of her face. Then his lips trailed a line of flame down to her throat, down, down in a silken burning path to the apricot tips of her breasts.

Wave after wave of pleasure swept her body as Alejandro slipped an arm under her shoulders to cradle her closer while his sweetly sensuous mouth drove her to heights of ecstasy she had not even dreamed were possible. In a helpless compelling flood of passion, April abandoned herself to him.

Alejandro touched her face, running his strong fingers through the fullness of the disheveled hair, which fell to her shoulders. He paused for a moment, looking deeply into her eyes, an expression of wonder on his face as he whispered her name. Then, with a low moan of desire, he pulled her into his arms.

When he moved his body over hers, she said, "No, your leg."

"I'll be careful. April," he breathed the name against her lips. "Oh, April."

Still she tried to hold back, tried not to give in to the sweet demands of her body. But, dizzy from the touch of his skin pressed next to her, she moved as he willed, and he eased her gown up over her hips, stopping momentarily to rip his pajamas open so that the hard-muscled length of him was against her.

The weight of his body half lying on her, and the scent of him filling her nostrils, intoxicated her. When his lips found hers, she shuddered with longing, her mouth welcoming him, her body softening under his as her hands moved across his muscular shoulders to bury themselves in his blue-black hair, urging him closer.

But he would not be hurried. He controlled her as he controlled the bulls he fought; he was enticing, elusive, taunting her until she ached with desire, trembled with passion. He waited until the waiting became an exquisite torture, till she gasped when she felt his maleness against her thigh. She felt a moment of panic when he moved to join them, but then caught her breath at the beauty of his darkly lashed green eyes looking down on her with such tenderness.

"My darling *gringa*," he murmured as in one fluid movement he joined his body to hers.

"Alec!" she cried softly, half in pleasure, half in fear, as he began to move against her. "Alec?"

"It's all right, April. It's all right, love. Love."

Sensation followed sensation. She closed her eyes when his hands tightened on her hips to draw her closer as he moved against her, carrying her on a sweet tide of desire that spiraled up and up until it was past bearing, until her body, frantic with longing, yearned toward his. "Alejandro!" She did not know whether she whispered his name aloud or not. Alejandro, my love, my love. Don't stop, darling. Don't ever stop. Oh, please, yes, please, yes, please.

Then, with a shattering intensity, his hands tightened on her body as together they tumbled over the precipice of passion, hands and mouths and bodies clinging as they whispered each other's name in the silence of the room and drifted down into the somnolence of soft reality.

Alejandro's head was buried in the hollow of her shoulder, her fire hair tumbled about his face.

With a tenderness April would not have thought possible, he caressed her breasts, the line of her hip, her back. Then he turned to kiss her love-bruised lips, to whisper, "I knew. I knew it would be like this, April. April mine."

Then they were silent, holding each other, content to lie close and warm.

And when at last he said, "Will you come with me to Pasajes?" she said, "Yes, Alejandro, of course."

Chapter 6

THE NEXT DAY THEY LEFT FOR SAN SEBASTIÁN AND Pasajes de San Pedro. April phoned her office in Madrid and told Pepita to tell Don Gustavo Alvarez, the head of the Madrid office, that she had decided to take a week of her vacation. She and Alejandro put her car in a parking garage, and with her behind the wheel of his silver-gray Mercedes coupe, they headed for the Cantabrian coast.

It was a lovely clear July day, and once they left Pamplona, they were in the midst of rolling green countryside. Stark white farmhouses, window flower boxes overflowing in a glow of color, dotted the landscape. Shepherds, wearing the black tams they had worn for centuries, tended their flocks in golden fields.

The road turned and twisted as they climbed higher, past meadows filled with wood sorrel and columbine, hollyhock and Queen Anne's lace. The top of the Mercedes was down, the July sun shown on their faces, and the sweet smell of summer was all around them.

When Alejandro's hand rested lightly against hers on the steering wheel, she stole a sidelong glance at his dark Gypsy face. The green eyes were covered now by sunglasses, his black thick hair whipped by the wind. She thought of how she had felt when he made love to her, of his passion and his tenderness. And of her response. She did not know how it would end between them. All she knew was that in the warmth of Alejandro's arms she felt a deeper joy than she had ever thought possible.

They drove into San Sebastián a little after one in the afternoon. April went slowly through the old quarter, maneuvering the Mercedes through streets crowded with summer tourists, following Alejandro's directions to La Concha Beach on the Bay of Biscay. They found a Basque restaurant facing the harbor and sat outside on the terrace. When the waiter brought the menu, April said, "You order for me," remembering how indignant she'd been that night at Botin's when Alejandro chose their meal without consulting her.

They began with a plate of charcoal-broiled sardines, then hearts of artichoke in a vinaigrette sauce, grilled prawns for her, stuffed baby squid for him. When April made a face over the squid, he insisted she try it, laughing when she asked for another bite—"Just to make sure"—then scooping a portion of it onto her plate.

When they left the restaurant, they drove along the Bay of Biscay to the small fishing village of Pasajes and found a hotel on the beach and a room with a balcony that overlooked the sea.

"This is lovely," April said. "I'm—I'm glad I came."

"So am I." He put his arms around her. "Would you like to swim?"

"Can you? I mean, won't it hurt your leg?"

He shook his head. "The salt water will do it good."

"All right. But later. You should have a nap."

"A nap! I haven't had a nap since I was four years old!"

"You're here to recuperate. It was a long trip, Alejandro. You need to rest."

He shrugged. "All right. If you rest with me."

"I'll sit on the balcony and read."

"I won't rest unless you do."

"You're behaving like a child!"

"Then humor me." With that oddly wry smile of his he headed for the shower. He came back, clad only in a terry wraparound that covered him from waist to mid-thigh. His body looked bronzed and fit. His shoulders were broad, his waist and hips narrow. His hair, still wet from the shower, gleamed as black as an obsidian sky.

April focused her attention on his leg. "You've taken the bandage off," she said in surprise.

"I always take them off as soon as I can."

Always. The word clicked in her brain.

As she let her gaze wander over his body, she saw the scars she hadn't seen before: one on his right shoulder; a thin red line across his ribs; a jagged, bunched mark that started at his waist and disappeared under the waistband of the wraparound. And then the still-red four-inch wound on his calf.

I'm not going to fall in love with him, April told herself when she stood under the shower, hoping that the water would wash away all the thoughts that skittered around inside her head. Thoughts of that slim, graceful body marred by scars.

She remembered that first Sunday in Madrid when he'd stood between the horns, his stomach and groin vulnerable as he dared the bull to charge him. She remembered and felt the sickness of fear.

Finally she turned the shower off, dried her body and

brushed her long auburn hair until it shone like a bright copper penny. Then she put on her short peach-colored robe and went into the room.

The balcony door stood open and there was a breeze from the sea. Alejandro had turned back the spread and the sheet and lay on his back, arms above his head.

"I'm almost asleep," he murmured as he reached for April's hand. Then with a sigh he closed his eyes.

April woke slowly, aware of the sharp clean smell of the sea and of gentle hands caressing her body. She sighed, half in a dream, half in awareness, carried along in a warmth of feeling, allowing a soft whisper of pleasure to escape when Alejandro's lips touched her breasts.

When she opened her eyes and reached to put her hands on his shoulders, he said, "No, April, lie still and let me make love to you." Then he bent to kiss her lips, tenderly at first, then with growing intensity, taking her lower lip between his teeth and into his mouth to tease it with his tongue. He bit the corners of her mouth, then soothed them with the lick of his tongue before he moved down the line of her jaw to her ears, to nibble with sharp little bites that drove her into waves of ecstasy before his lips traveled down her throat and moved to her breasts again.

Eyes closed, April let herself float on a sweet tide of emotion. She'd never felt like this, never even dreamed that anything could be like this. Complete surrender, aching desire, a longing to be so close to him that she could become a part of him so that her skin would become his skin, his bones her bones.

Gently he turned her on her side so that his head rested on her outstretched arm as he bent to kiss her breasts, first one, then the other, caressing the small peaked nipples with the warm moistness of his tongue and lips, teasing and kissing until her body burned with longing, until she whispered, "Alejandro, Alejandro, please."

He moved over her and covered her body with his. When he entered her, she moaned in delight, pulling him close, moving in perfect rhythm with him as her excitement mounted. And when her breath quickened, he sought her lips and whispered her name.

"I could make love to you for hours," he said. "I don't think I'll ever get enough of you, April. Never. Never."

When his hands went around her back to cup her buttocks and draw her closer, she lifted her body to his. Small moans of desire escaped her lips.

"I want to get lost in you," he whispered in a voice thick with passion. "I want to be covered by the softness of your body, the fire flame of your hair."

As the maleness of him moved within her, April's hands tightened on his shoulders and she cried his name and heard the hiss of breath in his throat. And together, clinging to each other as though they would never let go, they climbed the heights of ecstasy and tumbled breathlessly back to reality.

Slowly, gently, he caressed her back. Then his hands were in her hair, his fingers spread against her scalp as he pulled her to him so that his face was covered by the thickness of her hair.

And at last, when she lay in the curve of his arm, he said, "I think I knew the first time I saw you with Esteban that this would happen. I'll never forget how you looked that day, April. You were all in pink and you looked so unbelievably feminine and sexy." He kissed the side of her face. "I kept the hat so you would have to come and get it."

"I know." Her fingers curled in the black ruff of his

chest hair. "I only went to your apartment with Esteban because the hat was terribly expensive."

"You're lying."

She leaned on her elbow and looked down at him. "Yes." She kissed him softly on his mouth.

The sun was low on the horizon when they went down to the beach. They swam side by side for a long time and then went back to their room and showered and dressed for dinner.

They drove to San Sebastián and found a tavern with large smoked hams hanging from the wood-beamed ceiling, kegs of wine, brass pots, and red-checked tablecloths. They ordered paella, and with it they had thick slices of a richly seasoned garlic bread and red wine. When they finished, they went out to walk along the beach for a long time, watching the dip and drift of the fishing boats tied up at the wharf and the reflection of the moon on the water.

Finally they drove back to their hotel in Pasajes, to make love again and to sleep in the warm comfort of each other's arms.

The following day they crossed the border of France to Biarritz. After they'd had a cool drink, April browsed through a shell shop and Alejandro did some browsing of his own. That afternoon, when they had lunch at a beachside restaurant, he handed her a small white box, and when April opened it, she found a gold bracelet with a single charm, a tiny gold sea horse.

When she expressed her delight, Alejandro fastened it on her. Then, caressing the soft underskin of her wrist, he said, "We'll add to the bracelet, April. I'll buy you a charm so that you can remember every place I ever made love to you."

His hand tightened on her arm and his Gypsy eyes took on a smoldering, sensuous look. "I'm going to

make the bracelet so heavy with gold you won't be able
to lift your arm."

"Alejandro . . ." She felt caught by the hypnotic pull
of his eyes, helpless as the heat of his hand sent sparks
of desire through her body.

"I don't know what it is between us," he went on in a
voice so low she could barely hear him. "I only know
that I'll never get enough of you, that five minutes after
we've made love I find myself wanting you again and
that every time I'm near you, every time I touch you, I
want you."

He took a deep breath, released her wrist and in a
hoarse voice said, "Eat your gazpacho, for God's sweet
sake, and don't look at me with those warm cinnamon
eyes of yours or I'll drag you out of here right now."

This is insane, April thought. No word of love has
passed between us. He speaks of wanting me. And
yes—oh, God, yes—I want him. But I don't know why.
I don't understand what's happening to us.

It was late that night when they returned to their
hotel in Pasajes. The air was still, with just the barest
suggestion of a sea breeze, and because they had closed
the balcony door before they left that morning, the
room was stuffy.

When Alejandro said "How about a swim?" April
nodded and quickly changed to a strapless pale green
swimsuit and slipped her sheer turquoise beach robe
over it. When she had pinned her hair on top of her
head, she came out of the bathroom and announced
that she was ready.

The water was heavenly warm, the waves rising into
gentle swells. There were only a few lights reflected on
the water and no one on the beach or even on the hotel
terrace. They swam for a long time, and when they
came in to where they could touch bottom, April said,

almost in a whisper, "Everything looks deserted. It's like we're the only people in Pasajes."

"I wish we were."

"What would you do?"

"Make love to you on the beach."

"Like a savage, like a caveman," April said with mock severity, deliberately using the words she'd used that first night in Alejandro's bedroom.

"But that's what I am," he said, remembering, too, as their bodies moved together with the waves.

April lay back in the water so that she could look up at the sky full of stars, drifting as Alejandro drifted, letting the soft roll of the waves carry her. He kissed her, a lovely watery kiss, then pulled her into his arms and slid the green suit down to her waist so that he could touch her breasts.

It was a perfect night, April thought. A night she would remember for as long as she lived. She closed her eyes, shivering with desire as his hands peaked her to readiness. Then, because she wanted to delay the ecstasy that was to come, or perhaps because she knew that this perfect moment, like all perfect moments, would fade with the dawn, she pulled away from Alejandro and swam straight out. The salty sea breeze whispered against her face; the velvet water lapped against her body. Stroke after even stroke. Finding a patch of moonlight, she stayed within its shimmery beam, a part of the night, a part of the sea, which moved so sensuously against her bare breasts.

She heard Alejandro's voice behind her, and when she slowed and turned, he put his hand on her shoulder. "Don't run away from me," he said, and pulled her body close to his, hip against hip, leg against leg. Then, with a growl of desire, he wound his legs around hers and his hands cupped her buttocks, forcing her closer. He kissed her, his mouth against hers hungrily, his tongue searching and mingling with hers as together they sank beneath the water.

When they floated to the surface, he took her hand and they swam slowly back to shore. They were ten yards from the beach when all the lights at the hotel went off.

"It must be later than I thought," Alejandro said as their feet touched the sand and they waded out of the water. He handed April a towel. "You'd better take your hair down so it will dry," he said.

And when she did, ruffing it with a towel before she pushed it back off her face, Alejandro reached for her hand and led her farther down the beach, away from the hotel.

A small shiver of flame kindled in April's midsection when he spread his towel and pulled her down to the sand beside him. Before she could speak, his mouth was on hers and the length of his slick body pinned her to the sand. Then his mouth, so warm and tender, moved to her breasts, which were peaked with chill.

"Alejandro." Her fingers twisted in his wet hair as the small shiver of flame turned to a fire that coursed through every part of her body. When she gave a low moan of desire, Alejandro rolled away from her to pull his suit off, then hers.

Before the night air could cool the fever of her body, he began to kiss her, covering her face with small warm kisses that grew even warmer when they reached her breasts and moved to the soft white skin of her belly, the tender inner thighs. Only when she cried out in an agony of desire did he cover his body with hers.

Stars, bright and clear and brilliantly perfect, shown above them. The still night air caressed them as they moved rhythmically, perfectly attuned to each other's bodies as they whispered words of love and longing, words that turned to gasps of pleasure as their passions rose to a pinnacle of sensual delight.

Afterward they swam again, cleaning the sand from each other's naked bodies. April knew that for as long as she lived, she would never forget that night, or Alejandro, or the kiss of the waves against her skin.

They returned to the restaurant on the beach for a late lunch the next day. Alejandro seated April, then went around the table. He had just pulled his chair out when he saw the gray-haired man sitting alone at a table across the terrace. What caught his attention, he thought later, were the crutches leaning against the wall. As a waiter brushed by, he knocked the crutches aside.

"*Lo siento mucho*—I'm sorry," the waiter said, picking them up.

"*Está bien,*" the man said. "*No importa.*" He turned back to his glass of wine, and it was then that Alejandro saw he only had one leg.

"I am more clumsy than usual today," the waiter went on. "More wine, Señor Briviesca? A sandwich, perhaps?"

"Nothing, *gracias.*"

"Rufino?" Alejandro's face went white. "Rufino?"

The man with the one leg swiveled in his chair. His eyes widened in surprise. "Holy Mother," he said softly. "Is it really you?"

He tried to get up, and when he did, he lunged forward to grab the table to keep from falling. But Alejandro was at his side before he could fall, steadying him. He held the other man away to look at him. Then both men were clapping each other on the back, pretending the sea air had stung their eyes when they moved away.

Carefully, Alejandro eased his friend back into the chair. "I can't believe it," he said. *"Dios mío,* how long has it been? Five years?"

"Six. You were fighting in Málaga with Galan and the Mexican boy, Rivera. Curro Rivera."

"You're right. I'd forgotten. It's been a long time, *mano."* He turned and motioned to April, and when she came to him, he said, "I want you to meet someone. April, this is Rufino Briviesca, the best *banderillero* who ever planted the sticks."

"That was a long time ago," Briviesca said, taking April's hand. "A long time ago."

"May we join you?" Alejandro asked. "Or were you expecting someone?"

"No, I am alone, *Matador.* I am happy to have you and the young lady join me. What would you like?"

"Manzanilla for now, old friend." He hesitated, then, taking a deep breath, said, "Why didn't you let me know about the leg?"

"What was there to tell, Alec? It got infected and they cut it off."

A muscle jumped in Alejandro's cheek. "You should have told me, Rufino. You should have got in touch with me."

"You were in Mexico when it happened."

"But it was all right. I mean, after you recovered from the *cornada.* I tried to find you. I asked everybody I knew, but nobody knew where you were. You simply dropped out of sight."

"I was with my sister. She had a small farm near Córdoba. She died last year."

"I see." Alejandro turned to April. "Rufino was my

banderillero. He received a terrible horn wound in his right leg." He looked at the man sitting across from him. "You saved my skin that day. It should have been me that took the horn."

"Nonsense! I was careless and the bull caught me. It was time I retired anyway."

"But I thought your leg was all right."

"It was for a while. Then there was one infection after another. Then something with the circulation. By that time I was so tired of the damn thing I was glad when they cut it off."

"When did they do it?"

"Three years ago. I had an artificial leg for a while, but it wasn't any good."

"We'll get you one that is."

Rufino shook his head. "I'm all right the way I am."

"The new ones are very good," Alejandro said, brushing aside the older man's objections. He took a long sip of his Manzanilla. "What are you doing these days?"

"Nothing at the moment," Briviesca said after a slight hesitation. "But Luis Martinez—you remember him—he's after me to . . . to work on some sort of a deal with him."

"Tell him to forget it. You're going to the ranch."

Rufino glared at him. "The day has not yet arrived when I need charity from you or anyone else."

"Charity! For months I've been looking for somebody to manage La Esperanza. The man I had robbed me blind. I lost some good animals because of his stupidity. He had no more business on a brave-bull ranch than a street cleaner has. I've got to have somebody I can depend on, a man I can trust, or I'll have to sell the ranch."

"You're telling me the truth?"

"On my word as a gentleman."

There was a glimmer of excitement in the dark eyes. Then, with a sigh, Rufino shook his head and said, "I won't be able to do what needs to be done, Alec. Not the way I am now."

"You will once you get the leg. If it's all right with you, I'm going to send you to a man in Geneva. Pepe Vasquez told me about him. He'll fit the leg and keep you at his clinic until you learn how to manage. Then you'll be able to do as well as any man on the ranch."

Almost to himself Rufino said, "La Esperanza. The Hope. Perhaps I should not let you do this for me, old friend. A part of me says I am a proud man and that I must not accept this gift you offer, but the other part of me thinks how it would be to walk without those damn crutches. And to work with the bulls again, to ride out in the fields among them, to smell that wonderful odor of clover and manure . . ." He gripped Alejandro's arm. "I will work hard for you, *manito,* and I will never forget this."

"I'm not doing you any favors, Rufino. You'll work your tail off."

Alejandro clicked his glass against the other man's. "Here's to us. Between us we're going to make La Esperanza the best brave-bull ranch in Spain."

April watched them. Alejandro's face was alive with animation as he talked to his old friend. She judged Briviesca to be in his early sixties but thought perhaps he looked older because of what he had been through in the last few years.

She knew the two men had forgotten about her, but strangely she understood this need they had to talk of the bulls, of the *corridas* they had fought and of the men they had known.

They sat there all afternoon, forgetting to eat, drinking glass after glass of Manzanilla as they talked.

"Remember that Sunday in Mexico City? The bulls were from Tequisquiapan. And yours! What was his name, *Matador*? Ah, wait, I remember. It was Tiburón. The Shark, eh? With horns as sharp as a shark's teeth."

"Joselito Huerta fought with me that day," Alejandro said. "And Manolo Arruza. He'd just received his *alternativa*. He did a *quite por las afueras*, six or seven lances that were so good I wanted to kill him."

"And what about his *banderillas*, Alec? Like his father's, eh? Who would have thought we'd ever see another Arruza?"

The talk went on and on. At one point Alejandro reached over and took April's hand and kept it in his.

"Wouldn't you like to eat something?" she asked, but did not press when he shook his head.

Finally, when it grew dark, Rufino said, "I think I am very drunk, *manito*."

"And I, *amigo*." Alejandro signaled for the waiter and handed him some bills. Then he helped Briviesca up and handed him his crutches. "Where are you staying? We'll take you home."

"Not necessary. I can manage."

But Alejandro insisted, and they went out to the road and walked into the town where Rufino directed them to a mean waterfront cafe.

"I have a room here," he said. "It's just temporary, you understand."

"Pack tomorrow," Alejandro said. "We'll drive you to Biarritz as soon as I contact the doctor in Geneva. You can fly from there."

"There are no words . . ."

"Because between friends no words are needed," Alejandro said.

April took his arm when they walked back to their hotel. She knew that he was very drunk, but she knew why he was and so she did not speak of it. When they got back to the room, she helped him undress and get into bed. By the time she was ready, he was asleep.

She lay down beside him, but it was a long time before she herself could sleep. She thought of Rufino Briviesca and of how he had lost his leg in the bullring, of how old and tired he looked, how alone he was.

When she went to sleep she dreamed that Briviesca was in the bullring, fighting on his one leg. But as she watched he became Alejandro. April knew it was Alejandro because there was a bandage on his leg. Then there was no bandage because there was no leg, and then Briviesca, standing next to the *barrera* now, called out, "Do you see what happens when you play with the bulls, *Matador?*"

April came awake with a start, her body covered with perspiration, her hands knotted into fists. In her half-dream she reached out to touch Alejandro's leg to see if it was there.

Then, with her hand still touching him, she lay staring into the darkness of the room, afraid to sleep until the gray dawn streaked the sky and the shadows left the quiet room.

Chapter 7

THE NEXT DAY ALEJANDRO TELEPHONED GENEVA. HE spoke with a Dr. Schmidt, who set up an appointment with the man who would fit Rufino with an artificial leg. Arrangements were made for the ex-*banderillero* to remain in a clinic for therapy and for all bills to be forwarded to Alejandro.

"He'll be at the ranch in a month or two," Alejandro told April when they returned from putting Rufino on a plane in Biarritz.

"Do you really need him?"

"You always need a friend. Besides, he can keep Rafa company when I'm gone."

"Rafa?"

"My nephew. My sister's boy. I didn't tell you about him, did I? My sister and her husband were killed in an accident a year ago, when Rafael was thirteen. There were other relatives who wanted to take him, but he preferred to make his home with me. It's worked out well. He's a fine boy. He's almost ready to make his debut as a *novillero*."

"At fourteen? That's awfully young, isn't it?"

"I was fourteen when I started. Bullfighting is something you devote your life to, April." He hesitated. "Do you remember that first night we had dinner together at Botin's? When I told you then that I live to fight, that my profession is the most important thing in the world to me?"

"Yes, Alejandro, I remember."

"That's the way it has to be if you are truly to be good. You have to eat, drink and sleep the bulls. It is that way with me, and it will be that way for Rafa if he's going to be any good." Then, in a lighter tone, he said, "I hope you'll visit me at La Esperanza. I think you'll like it."

"You raise bulls there?"

"Brave bulls," he said with a slight smile. "There's a difference, you know. Fighting bulls are the product of hundreds of years of selective breeding. They're among the fiercest and bravest animals in the world. Wait until you see them in the pastures. When you come we'll ride out. They've got a strong herd instinct and won't bother you if you ride close to them as long as they're together. It's only when you separate a bull from the herd and enclose him in a small area that he becomes defensive and attacks. And once he's defensive, he's fearless. He'll attack a truck if it's in his way."

He ran a hand through his hair and with a grin said, "I'm talking too much. I always do when I talk about La Esperanza. I hope that once I retire it will keep me too busy to miss the ring."

"And when will you retire?"

"In eight or nine years."

"Eight or nine years!"

"I'm thirty-three, April. I've got some good years left." He reached for her hand and, changing the subject, said, "I apologize for getting drunk last night. I don't usually do that."

"I didn't think you did."

"It was a shock, seeing Rufino like that. I hadn't known about his leg."

"I understand."

"You should have seen him before. There wasn't a man in Spain as good with the *banderillas* as he was. No one was as fast or as agile."

And now he only has one leg, April thought.

She was quieter, more introspective, the following day, the day before they were to leave.

They swam and walked the beach, and when they came back to the room, Alejandro told her that he was well enough to fight in Valencia on the twenty-seventh of July.

"Will you come?" he asked. "You could fly in Friday and spend the weekend."

"I don't know, Alejandro. There'll be a pile of work waiting when I get back to Madrid, and I've got to go to Jerez de la Frontera before the end of the month."

"Jerez?" His face lighted up and he swung her off the floor and kissed her. "You can stay at the ranch!" he exclaimed. "I've got to go back to train so I'll be in shape for Valencia. This is wonderful, April. Just when I was beginning to wonder how in the world I could manage without you, I find I won't have to. You're going to be with me at La Esperanza. I'll arrange a *tienta* and—"

"Alejandro!" April looked at him, half annoyed and half amused, wondering how to make him understand that she worked for a living and that she wasn't free to leave whenever she wanted to. "I have a job," she said in a serious voice. "I can't take time off whenever I want to. I had a week's vacation coming; that's why I'm here now. I'll be going to Jerez to work, my friend. It's part of my job."

"Then quit your job."

"What?" She could not believe what he had just said.

"Quit your job. I'll take care of you."

April pushed him away, her face angry as she said, "I take care of myself, Alejandro. No one supports me. No one pays my bills."

"But I want you with me." His face was set and stubborn. "Your job isn't that important."

"Alejandro—" Hands on her hips, she stared at him. Then, trying to remain calm, she said, "I work for a living, Alejandro. And I like what I do. I'm good at it. It's important to me."

"And you're important to *me*. You care for me, April. I know you do. And in Spain, when a woman cares for a man, he comes first. Spanish women—"

"I've seen your Spanish women," she retorted. "Those women who hung all over you at your apartment. If that's the kind of a woman you're looking for, then you're welcome to her."

"That's not what I'm looking for and you know it." He put his hands on her shoulders. "I want you with me, April. I'm in a position to take care of you, to give you whatever you want. To buy you anything—"

"Buy me . . . !" April jerked away from him, her eyes blazing with anger.

She had expected anything but this, this offer to keep her. And although she hadn't known, hadn't really stopped to think where their relationship might go, his words came as a blow. She had given freely of herself with no thought of the future, content to be with him. She knew that she was in danger of becoming emotionally involved, yet she'd been unable to deny the intense attraction that had swept them together.

And he had said, "I'll take care of you. I'll buy you anything you want."

April faced him, white with anger as she said, "No! No, Alejandro. I won't live with you. How dare you even think—"

"You lived with a man before."

Her breath caught in her throat. In a low voice, her eyes never wavering from his, she said, "Yes, I lived with a man. But he didn't keep me, Alejandro. He didn't pay my rent or buy my clothes or pay my bills. I worked every day we were together."

His face tightened. "That's not the way it is in Spain. In Spain a man takes care of a woman he cares for. This week with you has been one of the most perfect times of my life, April. We're wonderful together. I want you with me. It doesn't make sense to me that we should be separated just because you have a job."

He reached out to pull her into his arms, but she backed away from him, still angry, and headed for the bathroom.

"Wait a minute. I want to talk to you."

"But I don't want to talk to you!"

"Don't turn away from me, *gringa.*" There was steel in his voice.

"And don't call me *gringa!*"

He pulled her against him, almost as angry as she was now, and held her in a captive embrace, his arms hard around her slender body. "Look at me!" he ordered.

"Let me go!"

"I said look at me, *gringa!*"

April did, her eyes spitting fire as she gazed into his.

"Don't ever turn away from me again. Don't try to

deny what is between us. And don't be angry that I
want to make you my woman."

"I won't be anybody's woman!"

"You'll be mine," he murmured as his arms crushed
her against him, as his mouth, hard and hurting,
covered hers.

And as April struggled against him, he looked deep
into her eyes and whispered, "You're my fire and my
flame, April. We belong together." Then, before she
knew what was happening, he picked her up and
carried her to the bed and yanked her bathing suit
down over her hips.

Hands curled into fists, as mad as she'd ever been in
her life, April struck out at him, twisting and turning as
she tried to get away. Struggling even as their bodies
joined. Crying out in anger and in passion, not sure
whether the nails she dug into his back were meant to
hurt or to excite. Feeling a thrill run through her body
when he gasped in pain.

"Damn you!" His voice was a low hiss of anger as he
thrust against her. His green eyes narrowed, his nostrils
flared, as his hands tightened on her shoulders. He held
her pinned to the bed by his muscled legs while his
mouth reached for her breasts.

"Don't!" April protested as his tongue flicked a
nipple. "Don't!" as his teeth scraped the delicate tip.
"Alejandro, don't!" even as she lifted her body to his.
And she did not know whether she cried his name in
defiance or in love.

He was blind with passion now as he moved against
her, his mouth devouring her breasts while she cried
out in protest and desire and fastened her fingers in his
thick black hair to pull his mouth up to hers.

Suddenly, still grasping her to him, he rolled onto his
back so that April was on top of him, his hands on her

waist, holding her, forcing her to move against him. Then his hands were in her fiery hair and he drew her face down to his.

"There'll never be anyone, anyone, but you," he whispered as she moaned against his lips, crying out as he thrust against her, rending her body, driving her to the edge of madness.

Then—oh, then—it was too much, and April sobbed his name against his lips and shivered in ecstasy when he said "My love. My sweet love" as together they toppled off the edge of foreverness.

His hands smoothed the hair from her face when she collapsed against his body. "You know," he said as he kissed her. "You know what is between us, love. You know I'll never let you go. My love. My love."

Pepita Rodriguez was the only one who knew April had been in Pasajes, but she did not know April had been there with Alejandro Cervantes until she glanced at the card that came with the bouquet of red roses that greeted April on her first day back at the office, the card that read "You know, my love" and was signed "Alejandro."

"Dios mío!" Pepita's small face was alive with excitement. "You've been with Cervantes!"

"If you tell anybody, I'll shoot you," April threatened.

"What is he like? I mean *really*. I knew he'd been hurt in Pamplona. Pamplona! Of course, you were with him there too!"

"Pepita—"

"Then it's serious between you. It must be, because in all the time I've known you, you've never had an affair." She wrinkled her nose and with a laugh added, "I've worried about you. I thought you were one of those coldhearted American women who thinks only of her career."

"I *am* a coldhearted American woman. But now and then I do think of something besides my career."

"Obviously." Pepita laughed. "What's he like?"

"Handsome."

"I *know* that!"

"Arrogant."

"An acceptable trait in a Spanish male. When are you going to see him again?"

"I'm not sure. Maybe this weekend."

"It's serious, then?"

"I don't know, Pepita. We're so different. It's difficult for us to understand each other. Alejandro can't understand why my job is so important to me, and I certainly don't understand his career. But I do know how important it is to him that nothing could ever interfere with it—especially not a woman."

"But would you want to interfere with it?"

"I don't know. But I don't think I could live with it." She tried to smile. "But there's no question of that anyway. We've never discussed a—a permanent relationship."

"Marriage, you mean?"

"Marriage, I mean." April took a deep breath and in a more serious voice said, "At the end of summer Alejandro will leave for a tour of Mexico and South America, and I'll be going back to the States before too long."

"I want to talk to you about that," Pepita said. "You know I asked if I could go with you."

"Yes, and it's all arranged. Señor Alvarez said he hated to lose you, but if that is what you want, he'd arrange it."

"That's just it, April. I'm not so sure now that I want to go."

"But the last time we talked about it, you said you'd definitely made up your mind."

"I know. But . . . but you see, Esteban and I have been seeing a lot of each other. I really like him, April. And . . ."

"And?"

"He's asked me to marry him."

"Marry him? Pepita, that's wonderful! I didn't know the two of you were serious. I knew you'd had a few dates, but marriage! I'm absolutely delighted."

"I haven't said yes, April. You see, I'm not sure I want to marry a man who grubs in the dirt for a living."

"Grubs in the dirt! Esteban's an executive and he's doing an important job. He loves working at the vineyard in Jerez; that's why he's there. He could transfer to the office here in Madrid tomorrow if he wanted to."

"But he doesn't want to. That's the problem." Pepita frowned. "Look, April, my father was a farmer until the day he died. He didn't even own a white shirt or have a pair of shoes that weren't caked with mud."

"But if he was doing what he wanted to do . . ." April tried to say.

"Oh, that's what he wanted to do, all right." Pepita's voice was bitter. "But it wasn't what my mother wanted. She came from one of the finest families in Burgos, April. They lost all their money in the Civil War and she had to leave the university. My father was a student too. She thought she was marrying a professional man when she married him. Instead, a year after the wedding, he bought a farm. She hated it, and when I came along, I hated it. I'll never live that way again."

"But Esteban isn't a poor man. You'd have a house in Jerez and—"

"I don't want to live in Jerez. I want to live in Madrid."

"I see."

"Esteban can take a job here in the office. Alvarez has offered to make him Vice-President in Charge of Foreign Sales. If he takes it . . . well, then I'll accept his proposal." Her look was defiant. "You don't approve, do you?"

"It's not up to me to approve or disapprove, Pepita," April said quietly. "But I think you're putting conditions on your love."

They did not speak of Esteban again that day. There was a lot of work for April to catch up on and a long report from the manager of the plant in Valdepeñas that needed her attention. Pepita helped her with the report, and as the young woman went through the previous years' figures, April studied her, wondering just how serious Pepita was about Esteban.

They were such totally different types. Esteban was tall and fair. The look of a Spanish nobleman was evident in his high forehead, clear gray eyes and large Spanish nose. Although he preferred working with his hands, there was no mistaking that he was a man of culture and breeding.

Pepita, like Alejandro, had the look of a Gypsy—an exceedingly voluptuous Gypsy. Only two inches over five feet, she had large, firm breasts, a tiny waist and flaring, seductive hips. Men would turn to look at her, and women tended to dislike her on sight.

When April chose Pepita as her secretary from among four or five candidates, several of the other women in the office voiced their disapproval. But April refused to waver in her decision. She liked Pepita's liveliness, her good-humored vibrancy. It wasn't any wonder, she thought now, that Esteban had fallen in love with her.

On Thursday morning Alejandro phoned from his ranch to ask April when she planned to leave for Jerez de la Frontera.

"Monday morning," she said.

"Driving?"

"Yes."

"I'd rather you didn't." And before she could say anything, he said, "It's a long trip from Madrid to Jerez, April. The highways are filled with summer travelers. I've made arrangements for you and Señorita Rodriguez to fly to Cádiz on Saturday. Esteban will meet your plane and drive you to the ranch."

"Now look here . . ." she said, beginning to bristle.

"Let me be a Latin male just this once, all right? Esteban's longing to see this Señorita Rodriguez, and the weekend will give them an opportunity to get together. He and I have planned a *tienta* on Sunday. Have you ever been to one?"

"No, but—"

"Then it's all settled." His voice was decisive. "Your plane leaves Madrid at seven–forty-five Saturday morning."

"Alejandro, I—"

"*Hasta luego,* April."

And before she could answer, the connection was cut.

Pepita was thrilled—more thrilled, it seemed to April, at the prospect of meeting Alejandro and of being on his ranch than she was at seeing Esteban.

But as soon as their plane rolled to a stop in Cádiz,

Pepita ran down the steps and across the tarmac to meet him. April, purposely allowing time for the two of them to greet one another, couldn't help smiling. Pepita made a striking picture in her bright summer dress, the short skirt swirling about her lovely legs, her high heels tacking against the pavement. Esteban kissed her, then held her away from him, his face shining with happiness as he smiled down at her. He gave his hand to April when she approached, saying, "*Buenos días*. Did you have a good flight?"

"Lovely," April said. "It's a beautiful morning."

"And it's going to be a beautiful weekend. Let's get your luggage and head for the ranch."

"How far is it?"

"A little over forty miles from Cádiz, but only twenty from Jerez. You won't have any trouble driving back and forth next week, April."

"So I'm staying at the ranch whether I want to or not!"

"You'll want to when you see it, and you know Alec wouldn't have it any other way." Esteban grinned at her. "I didn't know when I took you to see him fight that anything like—like this would happen."

"Like what?" she said, widening her eyes with pretended innocence.

Esteban laughed, then, with Pepita on one side and April on the other, headed for the baggage-claim counter.

La Esperanza, near the town of Lebrija, spread for what looked like to April to be hundreds of acres. The countryside was lush and rolling there, near the Guadalquivir River. Willows trailed leafy green branches through the clear cool water, grapes hung heavy on their vines and the fields were filled with yellow daisies.

As the three of them rounded the rise of a hill, they saw the bulls of La Esperanza.

Esteban slowed the car and said, "Magnificent, aren't they?"

"Dios mío!" Pepita said. "They must be worth a fortune."

"They are. Alejandro's proud of the ranch, even though he can't spend as much time as he'd like to here. But he will one of these days, when he retires."

"Where's the house?" Pepita wanted to know.

"A little farther along. We'll see it in a minute or two."

Then, even as Esteban spoke, they saw the house. It stood starkly white, except for the red-tiled roof, against the green hills. As they drew closer, they saw the graceful Spanish arches, the bright orange trumpet vines and the red bougainvillaea that covered one side.

"Alejandro bought the house and the ranch five years ago," Esteban said. He stopped the car in front of a circular drive and gave a light tap on the horn. They heard a shout and saw Alejandro running down an open corridor toward them.

"Hola!" he shouted. "It's about time you got here."

Dressed in tight jeans and a blue shirt that was open to the middle of his chest, he had to be, April thought, the most virile, attractive man she'd ever seen. He might be arrogant, macho and chauvinistic, but he was magnificent.

Behind him a tall, lanky boy came more slowly along the corridor. His skin was lighter than Alejandro's, his hair curlier and longer.

Pepita jumped out of the car first, and when Alejandro took her hand, he said, "Esteban has told me about you, Señorita Rodriguez, but he didn't half do you justice. Welcome to La Esperanza." And to Esteban he said, "Was the plane on time? No problems?"

"Everything was fine, Alec." He took April's hand and helped her out of the car.

Alejandro leaned to kiss her lightly on the lips. "Welcome to your home, *gringa*," he said softly.

The boy, who stood hesitantly behind Alejandro, frowned and looked away. But he stepped forward reluctantly when Alejandro said, "Rafa, this is the Señorita Rodriguez and the Señorita Juneau from the United States."

"How do you do." The boy put his hand out and gave each woman's hand a fast pump.

"Rafa's my right-hand man." Alejandro put his arm affectionately around the boy's shoulders. "I don't know how I'd manage without him. He's done most of the work arranging the *tienta* we're going to have tomorrow, and he'll be helping Esteban and me test the cows."

The boy bit his lip in an effort not to smile.

"That's wonderful," Pepita said. "And you're so young."

"I'm fourteen."

"I didn't mean *young* young," she said. "I meant young compared to your uncles—and to be doing such important work! Imagine: only fourteen and already you're fighting the bulls. That's very exciting, Rafa. Every woman in Spain will be after you in another few years."

He blushed scarlet and bit his lip again. "I'll carry your bags for you if you like," he said.

"Thank you, *querido*. And you can show me to my room. I'd really appreciate that." She flashed a smile at the others and said, "I'll see you later."

"Would you take Miss Juneau's bag too, Rafa?" Alejandro asked.

A slight frown drew the boy's dark brows together before he replied, "Of course, *Tío* Alec." And with barely a nod to April he muttered, "This way, please."

They followed him into a large open patio. There was a fountain in the center, which bubbled a light stream of water and was banked by full leafy-green ferns. Other green plants enclosed the patio, and through arched open doors April could see a large living room and a glassed-in dining room. At one end were curved wrought-iron stairs that led to the second floor where rooms opened off a balcony.

"This is lovely," April said as she looked about her. "You must love it here, Rafa."

He shrugged his thin shoulders and, without answering, led them up the stairs to the second floor. When he stopped before one of the doors, he said, "This is your room, Señorita Rodriguez."

"Pepita, *por favor,* or I'll think you don't like me," she said, her lower lip sticking out in a pretty pout. "All right?"

He nodded. "All right."

"Then say it."

"Pepita." He blushed.

"That's better. Thank you for carrying my bag, dear. I'll see you later." Then, turning to April, she said, "Why don't you knock on my door when you've changed?"

When April nodded and said that she would, Rafa picked up her bag and proceeded down the corridor. When he stopped outside the room that was to be hers, she opened the door and preceded him in. "Thank you, Rafa," she said when he put her suitcase down.

"De nada."

And before she could think of anything else to say, he turned and left the room.

April frowned at Rafa's retreating figure. She enjoyed young people, and usually they liked her. But this boy didn't, and she wondered if it was because he had seen Alejandro kiss her. But as she turned back to the room, all thoughts of Rafa fled.

The room was large and light, flooded by the noonday sun, which filtered in through open floor-to-ceiling French doors. The walls, like the walls in the rest of the house, were white. But everything else in the room was the palest, most delicate shade of pink that April had ever seen: thick, heavenly soft carpeting, a lush velvet chaise and ottoman, brocade drapes and a matching spread that covered the wide bed. Even the huge bouquet of roses on the dressing table were a deep pink.

April's eyes widened. It was obvious that everything was new. The carpet looked as though it had never been stepped on.

Had Alejandro redecorated the room just for her in her favorite color, pink? Her face flushed with pleasure. It was so obviously her room.

From the still-open door Alejandro said, "Do you like it?"

"Like it? Oh, Alejandro, it's beautiful."

"It's your room, April. I meant it when I said welcome to your home."

He took her hat and purse out of her hand and tossed them on the bed before he pulled her to him, resting his face against the top of her head as he rubbed his chin on her hair.

Through the open French doors came the sudden poignant song of a bird, flooding the room with its loveliness. Alejandro's arms tightened around her. Then his lips sought hers.

His kiss was a kiss to get lost in, April thought; his arms were a haven, a blessed homecoming. And suddenly, in that moment, she knew that she loved Alejandro Cervantes, that she had loved him since that first night at the party in his apartment. Her hands tightened on his shoulders and she leaned her head against his chest, afraid to let him see what she was feeling.

But Alejandro felt the strain of her body and held her away from him, a puzzled expression in his eyes. "What is it?" he asked.

April shook her head, not trusting herself to speak.

He kissed her eyes, her nose, her lips. And finally, when he let her go, he reached in his pocket and pulled out a small package. Handing it to her, he said, "I almost forgot this."

With trembling fingers April untied the pink ribbon and opened the box. Inside, wrapped in tissue, was a small golden bull.

"For your bracelet," Alejandro said with a grin.

"But we haven't . . ." She felt hot color flush her cheeks.

He laughed and kissed the tip of her nose. "But we will, my love. We will."

He let her go when there was a knock at the door, and a woman's voice called, "It is I, Luisa. I have come to help the *señorita* unpack."

"Come in, Luisa." To April he said, "We'll have some coffee and then I'll show you and Pepita around the ranch."

"All right," April said. When he had gone, she went into the adjoining bathroom to freshen up, then changed to form-fitting jeans and a soft yellow suede shirt, grinning at herself in the mirror when she tied her long auburn hair back from her face, thinking, I love him! I love him! I've never been so happy. I wish I could capture today. I wish I could keep it forever so that whenever I'm sad I can take it out and look at it and remember exactly how I felt when I knew that I loved Alejandro.

Chapter 8

"I HAVE SOMETHING TO TELL ALL OF YOU," ESTEBAN SAID that night at dinner. "I've decided to leave the plant in Jerez."

"Leave the plant?" April looked at him with concern. "But why, Esteban? I thought you were happy there."

"I was. I am. But I've decided to transfer to the Madrid office. I talked to Señor Alvarez and that offer of his, the job of Vice-President in Charge of Foreign Sales, is still open." He looked at Pepita. "I've accepted it."

"Oh, Esteban! Darling! I'm so glad."

He smiled his gentle smile and, taking her hand, said, "Now I have something else to say to you that can't be said here." He stood up and pulled her chair out and, taking her hand, said to the others, "Please excuse us."

"What's that all about?" Alejandro asked.

"He's going to ask her to marry him. And this time she's going to say yes," April said with a smile.

"Marry him! I'll be damned. I've never known

Esteban to be that serious about a woman. Marriage! Good Lord, I hope he knows what he's doing."

April stared at him, barely resisting the sudden urge to pour her glass of red wine over his head. Marriage is what usually happens when two people are in love, she wanted to snap. It's a natural progression.

At least it was for her. For as much as April considered herself a "modern woman," in her mind love was inextricably linked with marriage.

She lay awake for a long time that night, waiting for the sound of Alejandro's footstep outside on the balcony.

A footstep that did not come.

The guests for the *tienta* began arriving at seven o'clock that morning. By the time April dressed and went down to breakfast, there were fifteen people gathered in the dining room. Esteban and a radiant Pepita called to her and introduced her to Alejandro's friends.

"Alec and Rafa are already at the bullring," Esteban told her. "Help yourself to breakfast, and as soon as you finish we'll all go down. Carlos arrived late last night."

Alejandro's cook, as a concession to the guests who had traveled for several hours, had prepared more than the usual Spanish breakfast of coffee and rolls. There were cheese and potato omelets, which the Spanish called *tortillas;* sausages; quantities of hot, fresh bread; a fresh fruit salad; and *café con leche*.

By the time they arrived at Alejandro's bullring, most of the guests were seated. Others stood behind the *barrera*, the wall that circled the ring, and April went to stand with them.

She glanced toward Alejandro at the opposite side of the ring. Today he wore a *traje corto*—the high-waisted pants with the short, tight jacket and a white shirt that was open at the neck. There was a look of intense concentration on his face, and April suddenly realized that this was very serious business.

"Tell me about this," she said to Esteban. "Explain it so that I'll understand what's going on."

"All right. In the first place the word *tienta* means to prove or test. That's what this is all about. Besides using the ring to train, it's very important for a *ganadero*, a rancher like Alec, to test the bravery of the cows that will be used for breeding. The selection of the young cows today will determine the bravery of the bulls that will fight three or four years from now. All of Alec's prestige as a *ganadero* depends on selective breeding. A brave cow makes a brave bull.

"Everything that happens today will be recorded in a ledger: every characteristic of each cow, the number of times she attacks the *picador*, the way she follows the cape, the number of charges. Only trusted friends are permitted to see a *tienta*, April. The information is guarded and the results are private. A lot depends on today and on the absolute honesty of the reports that will be noted in the ledger."

Suddenly Alejandro called *"Silencio!"* then *"Puerta!"*

A cow ran into the bullring, eyes alert for danger, head high. It stopped, saw the horse directly across from it, lowered its head and charged.

"Wonderful," Esteban whispered as the cow butted the padded horse, trying to unseat the rider even as the steel-tipped lance jabbed her.

At last the animal pulled away, only to return again,

determined to attack regardless of the pain, until Alejandro ran into the ring shouting "Ahaaa!" to lure her away.

No one spoke when he began to test the cow with the *muleta*. The only sounds were the rush of hooves against the earth and the soft "Ahaaa!" as Alejandro called the cow for pass after pass.

"Do you understand how good Alec is?" a low voice asked.

April turned to see Alejandro's manager, Carlos Manzanares. His eyes, so brown they were almost black, looked into hers with a penetrating intensity. "Do you understand that a *matador* like Alejandro comes along once in a lifetime?"

"I don't understand as much as I should," April said quietly. "But yes, Señor Manzanares, I realize that he's very good."

"To be as good as he is takes total dedication."

"Most things do, don't they?" she said. "Whatever the profession."

He shook his head. "I'm talking about total dedication, Señorita Juneau. A *matador* is different from other men, just as a premiere ballerina is different from other women." His eyes narrowed. "I know that's difficult for you to understand, since you are an American, but a Latin would know what I am talking about."

April's hands tightened around the *barrera*. "Perhaps I understand more than you think, Señor Manzanares. I am curious about two things though: Why are you telling me this, and why do you dislike me?"

"Dislike you? My dear Miss Juneau, I don't even know you."

And you don't want to know me, April thought, as

with an abrupt "Excuse me" Manzanares turned his back on her.

The young matador from Valencia took the next animal, then Esteban tried his hand. He made several good passes before the cow caught him and barreled him to the ground. But before the horns could reach his body, Alejandro lured the animal away with his cape. Esteban, his face flushed, jumped to his feet and with a laugh waved Alejandro out of the ring so that he could continue to *torear*.

Rafa was next. He wore a *traje corto* that was an exact copy of Alejandro's. The young-boy look had disappeared; his face was tense and serious as he called the cow and led the animal gracefully past his body.

April, glancing at Alejandro, who was closer now, saw both the pride and the anxiety on his face.

"He's good, isn't he?" he said to Esteban. "Look at the way he holds his body. How steady he is. He's going to be a natural, *mano*."

"But I don't like the cow, Alec."

"Neither do I. I'll take her and Rafa can take the next one."

The cow that Rafa was fighting was small but feisty. She had sharp horns, and it was obvious that she needed an experienced hand. But when Alejandro called out "Let me take her," Rafa ignored him.

"Come on, Rafa," Alejandro said. "She's a holy terror. I'll finish her and you can have the next one."

"No!" the boy said stubbornly.

The guests were silent, sensing the tension between the boy and his uncle.

April glanced at Alejandro. His face was white, strained with tension, his body tensed to spring into the ring. When one of the men standing next to her uttered a muffled oath, she whispered, "What is it? Can he be hurt?"

"Of course! The great Belmonte suffered the most serious goring of his life from cow horns like those."

She glanced quickly at Alejandro and saw the whiteness of his knuckles as he gripped the edge of the fence. Following his gaze to Rafa, she saw the boy begin a pass to pull the cow closer. Too close. For suddenly the slashing cow-head rammed against Rafa's body. A horn hooked him, lifted him and, as the guests cried out, slammed his young body to the earth.

Alejandro and Esteban leaped into the ring, Carlos and the boy from Valencia one step behind them.

"I'm all right," Rafa cried, trying to struggle out of Alejandro's arms. "Goddamnit, put me down!"

His face was white and angry. Blood streamed from a wound in his arm. But when Alejandro carried him outside the ring and laid him down on the grass, he tried to struggle to his feet.

"I'm all right, Uncle Alec," he said. "That's my cow. I want to test her."

"You're not going to test anything today," Alejandro said. "Esteban's going to take you back to the house and phone for a doctor."

"Later, *Tío.* I can finish with the cow. Then I'll go back to the house. The arm isn't bad, it's just—"

"That's enough!" Alejandro motioned to Esteban. "Take him back and phone Dr. Larañaga. I'll be along later." And to Rafa he said, "You'll do exactly what the doctor tells you to do. Do you understand?"

Rafa glared at him. In spite of the seriousness of the wound, April had to suppress a smile, because nephew and uncle were so alike. So arrogantly male, each so determined to have his own way. But Alejandro dominated the boy—for now—and the boy, although it was obvious that Alejandro was his idol, hated being dominated.

The rest of the morning was spent testing the animals, but during the afternoon the guests that wanted to were allowed to take a turn with the *muleta*. And Pepita, in spite of Esteban's objections, was one of them. With Alejandro, Esteban and the young *novillero* standing by, she raced into the ring, the red cloth extended, her face glowing with excitement. Dressed in tight white cords and a red silk shirt, her black Gypsy hair streaming down her back, she made a vividly lovely picture as she stamped her high-heeled boots and called the animal to her, laughing with delight, her white teeth sparkling against her dark skin, her voluptuous body swaying gracefully as the cow swept past.

"Careful," Esteban warned nervously. And when April glanced at him, she saw the adoration on his face. His expression was so intense, the love that shone there so profound, that it frightened her. Love makes you too vulnerable, she thought sadly, knowing that the fear she felt was as much for herself as it was for Esteban.

A half-dozen tables were set up around the patio fountain. Candelabra glowed from wall sconces, and small candles floated in trays filled with gardenias in the center of each table.

April, not quite sure what one wore to a Spanish fiesta, had decided on the more simple of the two party dresses she had brought with her, a silky sheer strapless turquoise sheath that was covered with a chiffon float of an even paler shade of turquoise. She wore her auburn hair up, allowing loose tendrils of it to escape around her ears, and her only jewelry was the charm bracelet that Alejandro had given her.

She knew she had chosen correctly when she started down the wrought-iron stairs that led to the patio and saw the expression in his eyes as he hurried to meet her.

"It really isn't fair that you should be so beautiful," he said.

April squeezed his hand, and as he turned with her toward the other guests, she saw Carlos Manzanares watching her with his cold black eyes.

"How is Rafa?" she asked, looking away from Manzanares.

"He's all right. The doctor stitched up his arm and gave him a tetanus shot. His pride is hurt more than his arm. And he's angry because he can't come down to the party."

"Poor baby."

"He's not a baby, April. He's almost a man. A man who wants to be a *matador*."

"Don't sound so tough. I saw your face today when he was fighting. I know how terrified you were."

"Terrified?" His look was sardonic. "I'm never terrified, *gringa*. Except perhaps of you."

"Don't call me *gringa!*"

"Behave yourself. I'd hate to have to take you over my knee in front of all my guests."

"You impossible chauvinist!"

"You irresistible American." He handed her a glass of champagne from a passing tray and, with his arm around her waist, led her to a group of his friends, turning to welcome Pepita and Esteban when they joined the group. Pepita, in a white jersey gown that clung to her shapely body, plucked a gardenia from one of the centerpieces and stuck it behind one ear.

Champagne glasses were filled and refilled until finally Alejandro said, "The cook tells me that if we don't eat soon, her dinner will be ruined. Shall we start?"

"One moment, Alec," Esteban said. "I have an announcement to make and I think this is the proper time to make it." He put his arm around Pepita. "I—we . . . that is . . ."

"We're engaged!" Pepita said with a joyous laugh.

"That calls for more champagne," Alejandro said, clapping Esteban on the back. "The cook and the dinner will have to wait." He kissed Pepita's cheek and said, "Esteban's a lucky man."

Then it was April's turn to kiss her friend, to hug Esteban and join the others in drinking a toast to their happiness.

The mood that night was joyous. Toast after toast was drunk to the smiling couple. It was after ten before the guests sat down to dinner and long after midnight before the ones who were driving back to Seville bade their farewells. Only Carlos Manzanares was spending the night.

It was quiet in the patio after the guests had gone. One of the guitarists stayed behind, a bottle of champagne beside him, ignoring them while he played, as though for himself, some of the most beautiful classical guitar music that April had ever heard. Over near the fountain Carlos and Alejandro were talking, while April, Pepita and Esteban sat quietly at one of the tables.

"You really surprised me, you know," April told them. "I had no idea until last night that you were planning to marry."

"We'd have been married before this," Esteban said. "But Pepita was hard to convince."

"No, *querido*," Pepita said, "you were the one who

was stubborn. I thought you would never leave Jerez."
She reached for his hand. "We'll have fun in Madrid,
Esteban. We'll get an apartment near the Gran Vía
and—"

"In the heart of the city? I thought we could find
something a bit farther out."

"No, *mi amor*. I'm a city girl now and that's where I
want to be." And although she smiled and her fingers
played with his, there was a touch of iron in her voice.

Esteban smiled at her and then with a wink at April
said, "What am I to do, April? This *muchacha* has
wrapped me around her little finger."

So it seems, April thought, but did not voice the
words. Instead she pushed her chair back and with a
yawn said, "I'm going to say good night now. I'd like to
leave for Jerez at eight-thirty tomorrow morning,
Esteban, if that's not too early for you."

"No, that's fine, April." He stood to kiss her cheek.
"Sleep well."

"You, too, dear." She bent down and hugged Pepita.
"I'm so happy for you both," she said softly. "I wish
you all the joy in the world."

Then, because Alejandro was still deep in conversation with Manzanares, she simply waved in his direction
and went up the curved stairs to her room.

She felt curiously let down and was not sure why.
She'd been so delighted the day before by the warmth
of Alejandro's welcome, then surprised when he had
not come to her room. She was not sure whether it was
his dismay—a normal male reaction, perhaps, when she
told him that Esteban was going to ask Pepita to marry
him—or that he had wanted to be rested for today's
tienta.

He'd barely had time for her that day. He'd been
busy with his guests and the *tienta*. But even that night

he'd spent more time with Carlos Manzanares than he
had with her.

With a sigh April started down the corridor to her
room. She passed the girl Luisa and on impulse asked,
"Which room is Rafael's?"

"At the end of the corridor, *señorita.*"

"Has he eaten?"

The girl shook her head. "Nothing since breakfast.
That is not like him."

"Will you come down to the kitchen with me? Let's
see if there is something left from dinner that we can
fix."

With Luisa's help, because April was not familiar
with the kitchen, she heated up some of the paella and
fixed a fresh fruit salad. To this she added three
strawberry tarts and a glass of milk. When everything
was arranged on a tray, she told Luisa she could
manage and went back to Rafa's room.

"Quién es?" he called when she knocked.

"April Juneau."

There was a moment of silence before he said, "I'm
sleeping."

April smiled, put the tray down on the railing and
opened the door. "Do you always sleep with the light
on?" she asked cheerfully, picking up the tray as she
went into the room.

He slouched down in his bed, frowning when he saw
her.

"You look like your Uncle Alec when you frown like
that," she said. "I thought you might be hungry."

"I'm not."

"Just angry. Is that it?"

When he glared at her, she walked over to the bed
and said, "Sit up properly." Then she placed the tray
across his lap.

He looked down at the steaming hot paella and his nose twitched.

"I'm going to stay right here until you eat," April warned.

"Then I suppose I have to."

"I suppose so." She pulled a chair up close to the bed. "How's the arm?"

"It's all right."

"I thought you were very good today, Rafa." And when he raised his dark brows as though to say "You're a woman, what do you know?" she added, "And so does Alejandro. I heard him say so."

The young face brightened. "Really?"

"Really."

He didn't speak again until he had finished the paella and the fruit salad. Then he said, "Is the party still going on?"

April shook her head. "All of the guests left. But the others are still downstairs."

"Why aren't you?" A tone of belligerence crept back into his voice. "I thought you were so crazy about my Uncle Alejandro."

"I am crazy about him," she said calmly. "But I was tired and I wanted to see if you were all right." She reached for a tart and bit into it. "Umm, these are delicious."

"Where do you know Uncle Alec from?"

"I work with Esteban. He introduced us."

"You work?"

"Yep." She glanced at the tray. "The second tart is yours. I have to watch my figure."

"Your figure's okay."

"Thank you." She waited until he finished the second tart and his milk and then said, "Are you ready to sleep now? It's very late. Do you need to take a pill or anything?"

He shook his head and slid down in the bed. "Uh . . . Señorita Juneau?"

"Do you suppose you could call me April?"

"That's a funny name."

She smiled. "That's what your uncle said too." She reached down and smoothed the black hair off his face. "Good night, Rafa. Sleep well."

She was at the door when he said, "Hey, April. Uh . . . thank you for bringing me the paella and everything."

"You're welcome."

"Will I see you tomorrow?"

"I'm going to the office in Jerez with Esteban, but I'll be back in the afternoon. Is there anything you'd like me to bring you from Jerez?"

"No, thanks."

"Good night, dear."

"Good night, April."

She felt better than she had all evening, she thought as she showered and got ready for bed. She was glad she'd spent a few minutes with Rafa. If she and Alejandro were to form any kind of a permanent relationship, she wanted the boy to like her. She remembered from her own growing-up years that being fourteen wasn't easy. And it must be doubly difficult for Rafa, who had lost both his parents.

After she had brushed her hair, she looked in the dresser drawer for a nightgown, but instead, when she opened the drawer, she found a tissue-wrapped package.

She opened the tissue and gasped in delight as she held up the sheerest, loveliest nightgown she'd ever seen. It was made of yards and yards of pink chiffon, and when she slipped out of her robe and put the gown on, it slid over her body like a silken caress. Soft elasticlike lace held it low over her shoulders, outlining her breasts and billowing in a cloud about her body.

Hugging her arms, April shivered with delight and moved to the mirror to study her reflection. She loved beautiful lingerie, but this was surely the most extravagantly pretty gown she'd ever had.

Once again she picked up the hairbrush and brushed until her long red hair fell in shimmering waves down her back. Then she dabbed perfume behind her ears and between her breasts, turned off the light and slipped into bed.

Moonlight streamed in through the partly open French doors. From across the room she could smell the scent of Alejandro's roses. Suddenly she heard a step and saw a shadow silhouetted against the fluttering white curtain and heard the murmur of her name.

He moved into the room and sat on the side of the bed, looking down at her. "I've had too much wine," he said.

"We all have."

"I just looked in on Rafa. He said you'd taken his supper to him. That was nice of you."

"He was upset over what happened today." She hesitated. "Do you think that he really will be a *matador*, Alejandro?"

"I'm afraid so."

"Why afraid, Alejandro?"

"You're always afraid for the people you love." He reached out and touched her hair. "Carlos thinks I'm falling in love with you."

April felt the breath catch in her throat. She tried to speak but no words came.

"He's wrong, April. I'm not *falling* in love with you. I am in love with you."

"And you're not sure you want to be," she said in a low voice.

He looked stunned as she said, "I know, darling. I know you'd much rather have fallen in love with a proper Spanish lady, one who would sit quietly in the background of your life, never argue and never threaten to kill you if you even so much as looked at another woman." She sat up and, touching the side of his face with her fingers, said, "Poor Alejandro. In love with this terrible American."

"Damn you!" With a growl that was half in jest and half in anger, he pulled her to him, kissing her with a ferocity that almost frightened her, crushing her to him in an embrace that left her breathless with desire.

When she managed to free herself, she laughed and said, "You'll wrinkle your gift."

"The gown? I'd almost forgotten. Does it fit?"

"See for yourself." She switched on the low light beside the bed. "Thank you, Alejandro," she said. "It's the loveliest thing I've ever owned."

"Then take it off before you ruin it."

Excitement stirred in her body. But before she could slip it over her head, Alejandro said, "Stand up so that I can watch you, April."

The pulse beat in her throat and she felt her excitement grow into a smoldering warmth as she slid out of bed and stood silently in the shadows. Then slowly, with trembling hands, she pulled the cloud of chiffon over her head and draped it across the bed.

"Lie on the chaise," he said in a low voice.

"What?" The word quivered on her lips.

"On the chaise, love."

His green eyes touched her body like a flame as she

crossed the room and sank down on the pink velvet chaise. He turned the light off. The room was flooded by a silvery shaft of moonlight. He undressed and came toward her and, with gentle hands, touched her hair and said, "My lovely *gringa*."

His hands moved slowly across her face as though memorizing her features before he stroked down her shoulders to her breasts. He touched them with tenderly erotic fingers that scorched her skin and kindled a fire that once started must surely burn to completion.

Hands of fire traced down her body to outline her hips, the tender inside of her thighs, moving slowly down her legs, then back to her belly before their warmth covered the crisp triangle of her hair.

"Alejandro," April whispered as he bent to kiss her breasts. But as she moved, almost unable to bear the passion rising within her, he said, "No, love. Lie still. Lie still."

He kissed her mouth, gently at first, then harder, deeper, while his arms went around her to urge her closer to him, her naked body tight against his as he whispered her name against the curve of her neck. Then gently he laid her back against the softness of the velvet and began again to kiss her—her eyelids, her cheeks, her lips, not letting her respond before he moved to nibble her ears.

"Alec, Alec, darling." Her body yearned toward his as his hands caressed her breasts and he bent to touch them with the warmth of his tongue.

"Please—oh, darling, please," April pleaded as he lay beside her, as he stroked the long, smooth length of her body, making her wait until the waiting became a special kind of torture.

With a low moan of need April sought his mouth, fierce and demanding, her body aflame.

"April," he whispered, "Oh, April," and joined his body to hers with heart-stopping intensity.

Wave after wave of pleasure swept her, carrying her higher and higher as he moved against her. And when she began to gasp with pleasure, Alejandro said, "Tell me. Tell me."

"I love you," she cried, and covered his mouth with hers. Then again: "Oh, Alejandro, I love you. I love you."

She felt the most consuming joy she had ever known when he whispered her name and shuddered against her in the ecstasy of completion.

Chapter 9

IT WAS STRANGE, APRIL THOUGHT, HOW QUICKLY ONE adapts to change. La Esperanza was different from any place she had ever known; yet, it seemed sometimes that that was where she had always been, that she had always awakened to the sunlight streaming across her bed, the sound of birds singing from the leafy-green branches of the pepper trees and the bubbling splash of water from the stone fountain in the patio.

And each morning as she lay on the chaise, drinking the *café con leche* that Luisa brought, feeling the sweet lingering fatigue that was the aftermath of a night of love, she knew that she was happier than she had ever been in her life.

She and Esteban drove to the plant in Jerez de la Frontera every morning. When they returned to La Esperanza in the late afternoon, they usually found Alejandro and Rafa—and sometimes Carlos—waiting for them on the patio. Alejandro's leg had completely healed, and he spent his days training for the coming fight in Valencia. He ran two miles every morning, combining his backward runs, sideways and zigzag runs with slow pacing and short bursts of speed. He practiced with both the *capote* and the *muleta* and worked long hours with the *carretilla*, the wheelbarrowlike apparatus with the padding and the horns that was used to practice the planting of the sticks.

Rafa trained with him, and though Alejandro did not speak of it, it was obvious that he enjoyed Rafa's companionship and that their relationship was more like father and son than uncle and nephew. With pride in his voice Alejandro told April how well Rafa was doing, how fast he learned. But there were moments, when Alejandro was not aware that anyone noticed, that he looked at Rafa with fear in his eyes.

Since the night that April had brought Rafa a dinner tray, his animosity toward her had disappeared and he had begun to treat her like an older sister. Sometimes they had long serious talks and other times they just had fun together. And Alejandro, watching them, would smile and say, "I'm not sure which of you is the teen-ager."

When Carlos joined them they dined on the patio, then sat for a long time over cinnamon-flavored coffee, enjoying the quiet time after the day's work was done. If Alejandro noticed that Carlos always addressed his comments to the males of the family, he did not speak of it. Nor did April. She knew Carlos did not like her and that he objected to her presence. It was something she did not know how to fight, and so she didn't even try.

Each night, when the house was still, Alejandro came to her room. He did not tell her again that he loved her, and although she longed to hear the words, she knew that there were people to whom the words of love did not come easily.

On Saturday they all flew to Valencia for the *corrida*

in which Alejandro would fight on Sunday. They found a restaurant overlooking the Mediterranean, and after they had eaten, Carlos said, "You haven't been getting your proper rest, Alec." His gaze skittered across April's face. "I hope that tonight you will."

Just for an instant a flash of annoyance tightened Alejandro's face. Then with a shrug he said, "Perhaps you're right, Carlos. There have been so many things on the ranch that needed attending to. I am a little · tired. We'll all make it an early night."

"I'd like to look at the bulls at the *sorteo* tomorrow morning, Alec. You can see your . . . April in the afternoon after the fight."

His hesitation before her name was slight. But Esteban noticed, and with a lift of his eyebrows he glanced at Carlos, then at April. But he said nothing until the *corrida* the next afternoon. Rafa had gone to look for a program, leaving April and Esteban alone for a few minutes.

"Has Carlos spoken to you about your relationship with Alec?" Esteban asked.

April nodded. "The day of the *tienta* he asked me if I understood how really good Alejandro is and how necessary it was that he be dedicated to his profession. He doesn't like me, Esteban, and I don't know why."

"I do." Esteban's face was thoughtful. "He's been with Alec since the early days, April. Theirs is almost a father-son relationship. Carlos sees Alec as the son he never had and as the *matador* he himself had hoped to be. Alec is a star, a perfect example of what a bullfighter should be. It's odd, April. Carlos has never objected before to the women that . . ." He hesitated, reluctant to continue.

"It's all right," April said. "Please go on."

"Well, Carlos has never objected to the women

who've always flocked around Alec. Even to the affairs Alec's had. I think he objects to you because he knows you're special, April. He knows you're not just another woman in Alec's life, that this thing between you goes deep. Carlos is afraid of you."

"But why?"

"You might take Alec away from him."

"Away from him! Esteban, I don't understand."

"You might make him quit the profession, April."

"But I'd never do that."

"Never say *never*, my dear. Most wives and mothers never see their men fight. They spend the whole *corrida* on their knees in a chapel, praying for their safety, dying a little every time their men step into the ring."

"But I wouldn't be like that, Esteban. I'd never interfere with Alejandro's career."

"I don't think you'd want to, April. But I wonder."

Rafa returned then, and a few moments later the band began to play *Gallito,* a favorite with the Spanish *aficionados.* Then came the sound of the trumpet, the large gates swung open and the *alguacil,* mounted on a sleek black horse, dressed in black velvet and wearing a plumed hat, rode into the ring to officially open the spectacle. Doffing his hat to the judges, he returned to the *puerta de cuadrillas* to the accompaniment of a *paso-doble.* Next came the glittering parade as the three matadors stepped into the ring, each followed by his *banderilleros,* the mounted picadors and behind them the *monosabios,* the men who helped with the picadors' horses. A team of gaily decorated mules brought up the rear.

Alejandro, in a blue and silver suit of lights, came to stand before the judges' box with the other two matadors. Then he moved to where April, Rafa and Esteban were and draped his colorfully embroidered parade cape over the railing. After one brief smile he turned away to make a few passes with his cape to loosen up.

In the meantime the *alguacil* had given the key to the *torilero*, who held it up to the authority, who in turn gave the signal for the gate to be open.

"Uncle Alec will be first," Rafa said. "He's the oldest in the profession today."

The music stilled. An expectant hush fell over the crowd. Alejandro stood below her, a yellow and magenta cape in one hand. His eyes were on the gate.

The shrill thin sound of the *clarín* split the air. The gate swung open to expose a low dark passageway. Then came the heavy thud of hooves and the deep-throated roar of the crowd as the bull exploded into the ring.

Alejandro dashed into the center arena, dropped to his knees and called, *"Ahaaa, toro!"*

The animal focused on him. Then, head down, muscled shoulders bunched to do battle, he charged the kneeling man.

There was a colorful swirl of cape as the bull passed close—oh, so close—to Alejandro's face, whirled to return and charge again, while all around the arena the crowd screamed their fright and approval as he jumped to his feet to execute three *verónicas*, which he followed with a *rebolera*.

A burst of music, the applause of the crowd, the shouted, *"Olé, Matador! Bravo!"*

April thought she smiled—and knew that the smile was stiff and forced, that everything in her body was frozen with a fear that was so real it was palpable. For surely her heart had stopped beating. Surely the blood had frozen in her veins.

Unable to look away, she stared at the slim figure in

the ring as he called the bull closer and yet closer as the stiletto horns reached for his body.

She did not realize that Esteban had spoken to her until he put his hand on her arm and said, "April? April, are you all right?"

She turned to him, smiling her stiff, terrible smile, and said, "Of course, dear. Of course." Then she turned back to see the two *picadors* enter the ring, almost unaware of what she was watching until they had come and gone and the crowd began to cry for Alejandro to plant his own *banderillas*.

"He's going to do it," Rafa said, excitement in his voice. "Nobody does the sticks better than Uncle Alec."

Alejandro glanced toward the *barrera*, nodded to Carlos, then motioned the *banderilleros* away, indicating that he would plant the three pair of sticks himself. Taking a pair of the bright barbs decorated with colored paper, he went to the center of the ring. He called the bull to him, provoked it to charge, then stood his ground, feet together, the colored sticks held at shoulder level.

The bull raced toward him. Alejandro ran to face the bull, and when the animal was almost upon him, the horns already lowered for the charge, Alejandro stepped out, feinted to his right—one foot still in place while the bull followed the direction of his right arm as Alejandro shifted to his original position—and placed the *banderillas*.

"*Olé, Tío!*" Rafa shouted, jumping to his feet. "*Olé!*"

Alejandro used the same maneuver to plant the next pair, but with the third pair he broke the sticks in half and went high up over the horns to place them.

April did not think she would ever breathe properly again. She couldn't bear to watch Alejandro, and she couldn't bear to look away. She sat quite still while he dedicated the bull to the crowd, listened to the music and watched the final third of the bullfight in a state of rigid terror.

When it was over, she said she had to go to the ladies' room and that—yes, indeed—she was quite all right and would be back in a few minutes.

With a fixed smile still on her face, April reached the rest rooms and the privacy of a small closed booth before she was sick. Finally, when her stomach was empty, she left the booth and a woman attendant, her face wrinkled with concern, handed her a wet towel.

April leaned against the sink, the towel to her face, trying with every ounce of her strength to control her quivering stomach.

"Sit, sit," the attendant said, pulling a stool from under one of the sinks.

"Gracias," April managed to whisper as she sat down and leaned her head back against the wall.

Never had she known such all-consuming terror as she had experienced during the previous fifteen minutes. Esteban had told her that wives and mothers of *toreros* did not usually attend *corridas,* but she hadn't really listened. She'd seen dozens of bullfights during the year she had been in Spain, and she'd seen Alejandro fight twice before that day. What had happened to her? Why was she behaving this way?

Then, suddenly and clearly, April knew: She knew, because she loved him, that it would be this way every time she watched him fight. The thought left her hollow. How could she live with this fear?

In a little while April washed her face, and reapplied her makeup, adding a bit more blusher than she normally used to cover her paleness. After she had thanked the attendant, she went back to the *corrida*.

She evaded Rafa's question when he asked her if she was all right. She greeted Alejandro after the *corrida* was over, laughed and joked and drank one more gin and tonic than she was used to. When Carlos Manzanares stared at her with his black appraising eyes, she stared back defiantly. She carried the dinner conversation, making Rafa laugh at some of her misadventures when she'd first come to Spain. "I told the butcher to slice the meat *despacio* instead of *delgado*, slower instead of thinner. My voice kept getting higher and squeakier. *'Despacio,'* I said, *'despacio,'* while the poor man looked at me as though I'd lost my mind and moved the knife back in forth in slow motion."

And no one, except perhaps Carlos Manzanares, noticed that she didn't eat, that she merely pushed her food around on her plate.

That night, when Alejandro made love to her, April lifted her body to his with an urgency that bordered on desperation, clinging to him as though she would never let him go.

Caught up in the passion of the moment, he didn't sense the intensity of her embrace. He only knew that her arms urged him closer and that her lips and her body seemed insatiable.

When it was finished he pulled her into his arms and told her how wonderful she was. And finally, still holding her, he fell asleep, cradling her to him.

But April lay awake for a long time, silent bitter tears streaking untouched down her face.

The next morning, when Alejandro, Rafa and Carlos went back to the ranch, April returned to Madrid with Esteban.

During the next few weeks she threw herself into her work. Alejandro fought almost every Sunday and sometimes, when there were festivals, during the week. When the *corridas* were close to Madrid, April would leave early Saturday so that she could spend the weekend with Alejandro and attend the *corrida* on Sunday.

They did not cease being painful, but she was able to hide the way she felt. She stayed very busy during the week, often staying at the office late in the evening. Occasionally she got together with Pepita and Esteban for a drink or dinner. But April knew that new lovers rarely need a third party and declined most of their invitations.

Esteban seemed to be doing well in his new position as Vice-President in Charge of Foreign Sales. But it was strange to see him in a business suit rather than the faded jeans and mud-caked boots he'd worn in Jerez. He came to the office early and stayed late. If he sometimes looked harried and out of sorts, April told herself that a new job always took some getting used to and that Esteban would adjust.

Alejandro returned to Madrid for a week in the first part of September. He told April that Rafa had started school, a boys' academy in Cádiz, and that he wasn't happy about it.

"He says *matadors* don't need to know geometry," Alejandro said. "The only class he likes is English. He's determined to surprise you by speaking to you in your own language." He grinned. "I think he's got a king-size crush on you."

"And I've got a crush on him," April said with a smile.

On his second night in Madrid, Alejandro invited Pepita and Esteban to join him and April at Botin's.

When they had ordered drinks he asked, "Have you set a date for the wedding yet?"

"It will be some time in November," Esteban said. "You'll be my best man, of course. April has already agreed to stand up for Pepita."

"When in November?" Alejandro frowned slightly.

"The first or second week."

Alejandro glanced at April, then said to Esteban, "Carlos has set the schedule up this year. We're leaving for Venezuela the third week in November."

"So soon? You didn't go last year until January."

"I know, *mano*. But Carlos handles these things."

And he wants you out of Spain, April thought, looking down at her plate. Alejandro was leaving and he had not told her. Suddenly she felt drained and tired. Voices buzzed around her and she didn't hear them.

"Have you ever been to South America?" Alejandro's hand touched hers.

"What?" Startled, she looked up.

"I asked you if you had ever been to South America."

"No. No, I haven't."

"Then I think you should come with me."

"I can't do that," she said.

"Why not?" His dark brows puckered in a frown.

"I have a job, Alejandro." She tried to summon a smile. "It's one thing to drive to Avila to see you fight. But Venezuela for a weekend? That's asking a lot."

"I didn't expect it to be for a weekend." His hand tightened on hers.

"What did you expect?" Her body stiffened with anger. He was leaving and he had not told her. Now he thought that she could drop whatever she was doing and go with him.

"I expect you to leave your job and come with me."

"I don't think Carlos would like that."

"What in the hell is that supposed to mean?" His green Gypsy eyes shot darts of anger.

"Listen, you two," Esteban put in, "if this is a private fight, Pepita and I will leave."

Alejandro flushed. "It's not a fight, Esteban. It's a . . . somewhat heated discussion. Let's have another drink, shall we?"

Then, with a tight-lipped smile, he said, "April and I can discuss this later."

Chapter 10

"I DON'T UNDERSTAND," ALEJANDRO SAID. "WHY IN THE hell can't you come to South America with me?"

"Because I have a job here and because I will *not* go traipsing around the world with you. And if you tell me one more time what a Spanish woman would do if she loved a man, I'll throw something."

Angrily they faced each other across his living room. He had not even asked her where she wanted to go after they dropped off Esteban and Pepita; he had simply driven to his apartment and swung the Mercedes into the parking garage, and when she had said, in a voice that dripped icicles, "I prefer to go home," he had replied, "And I prefer to have you here."

He came around to her side and, with a not-too-gentle hand, helped her out of the car. They didn't speak in the elevator, but once inside he turned on her angrily and said, "Now what in the hell is this all about? And what was that crack about Carlos? I know you don't like him, but—"

"*I* don't like *him!* The man hasn't been civil to me since the day we met and you ask me why I don't like him! He's rude and unpleasant and it's obvious to everyone but you that he can't stand me. I'm not surprised you're leaving for South America sooner than you expected; he wants to get you out of my clutches."

"Your clutches! That's crazy, April." He ran nervous fingers through his thick dark hair and in a calmer voice said, "Carlos and I have been together a long time. My father died when I was twelve. Carlos owned the ranch next to ours. He was my father's best friend. And he's been both friend and father to me for almost twenty years. I know he's difficult sometimes, but it's only because he has my best interests at heart."

"And I'm not in your best interests."

"Don't say that." Alejandro's voice lowered to a soft intensity. "I want you to come to South America with me, April. I thought you'd want to come."

She shook her head. "I can't, darling."

When he started to speak, she held up her hand as though to ward off his words. "No, please. Hear me out. I love you and I love being with you. But I won't live with you. I won't quit my job and let you pay my expenses. I'm sorry, but I value myself more than that."

"All right then, damnit, we'll get married."

April stared at him, angry tears stinging her eyes. "What a perfectly lovely proposal," she managed to say.

"Oh, God, I'm sorry. . . . Don't be angry, please. You know how I feel about you. I love you, you know that. I haven't said anything about marriage before because I promised myself I wouldn't marry until I retired. It was an easy promise to keep because there wasn't anyone who was important enough to me, anyone I wanted to spend the rest of my life with, until I met you."

He put his arms around her, nuzzling her hair with his chin. "This thing between us, April, it's happened so fast."

"I know." Her voice was so low he could barely hear her.

"I want what's best for you, *querida*. Being married to someone like me isn't an easy thing. You'd either live at the ranch or travel with me. I don't know which."

"I wouldn't want to stay at the ranch without you, Alec. If I kept working—"

"No, I wouldn't permit that."

April shoved him away. "One thing you'd better remember, Alejandro Cervantes, is never to use that word with me. If I do decide to marry you, we're going to be equal partners."

"Equal partners! Do you think this is a business? It's a marriage we're talking about, and in a marriage the man is the head of the family. I will always treat you with respect and love, but—"

April snatched her purse and jacket off a chair. "You're impossible," she shouted as she headed for the door. "I can't marry you. It would never work."

But Alejandro was only a step behind her, and just as she reached for the doorknob, he grabbed her and swung her around to face him. When April opened her mouth to speak, he covered it with his, crushing her to him, his chest hard against her breasts, his arms against her back to force her close to him. Then, before she realized what he was going to do, he swept her up in his arms and carried her to the bedroom, where he dropped her on the fur-covered bed.

"Let me go!" April struggled to sit up but he forced her back, his Gypsy eyes blazing with anger.

"One thing we're going to resolve right now," he said, "is that when we have a fight—or a heated discussion—you are not going to turn your back and walk away from me. And right now you're going to stay if I have to tie you to the bed."

"Damnit, Alejandro—"

"*Cállate!*" he thundered. "You *will* marry me. You *will* behave like a good Spanish wife. And you *will* go to South America with me."

"No, I won't!" She lashed out at him but he caught her hand in midair.

"Don't you ever try that again April, or you'll regret it. And believe me, because I mean it!" Then, trying to control his anger, he said, "I don't want it to be like this between us, but sometimes I don't know how to handle you. You're different from any woman I've ever known. Sometimes I get so angry I want to shake you, but most of the time I just want to—to love you."

April looked up at him, feeling her anger fade, and with a sigh she whispered, "What do you want to do now?"

His eyes met hers. "I'm not sure," he said in a husky voice.

"We're so different, Alejandro."

"I know."

"I'm not sure we can ever work out our differences."

"But we can enjoy trying." He unbuttoned her blouse, then pulled it off her shoulders and reached to unfasten the lace bra, resting his face against her breasts when he slipped it off.

"I'm not sure this is the way to settle an argument," April whispered, soothing the heavy black hair back from his forehead.

"I can't think of a better way." Alejandro pushed her back on the bed and took her shoes off, then began to slowly undress her. When she was clad only in her peach satin briefs, he looked down at her, at the red hair tumbled about her face, at the smooth ivory whiteness of her skin, the peaks of her lovely breasts, the gentle curve of hip and waist. Then slowly, his nostrils flared, his lips parted with desire, he pulled the peach satin down over her hips so that she lay naked against the fur. He watched her while he took his own clothes off, not speaking as he studied her body, caressing her with his eyes.

April felt the erratic thump of her heart as she looked up at him. It was as though she had no will of her own, she thought, that she was helplessly held against the softness of the fur spread, waiting for the bronzed man who stood above her to take possession of her body. A slow warming flame of excitement spread through her veins like hot liquid fire, and she whispered his name.

"Tell me," he said softly.

"I—I want you."

"What else?"

"I love you."

"And I love you, April. Always remember that. You're my love, my own, my only love."

He came down beside her, his arms around her back, the crisply curled chest hair tickling her breasts, the musk scent of him filling her nostrils as he buried his face in her hair.

When finally his lips found her mouth, he held her while his mouth devoured her, stopping only to kiss the corners of her mouth before he trailed moist kisses down her throat. At last he cupped her breasts, warming them with his hands as he kissed them, teasing them until she was pliant and trembling in his arms, until she reached up to pull his face to hers, to kiss him as deeply as he had kissed her.

Slowly, lingeringly, April let her hands roam the length of him, feeling the smooth hard muscles with her fingertips as she trailed down his back to the curve of his buttocks. Finally her arms went around his shoulders as with a fierceness she had not known she possessed she kissed him, wanting to consume him as he had consumed her. She lifted her body to his, demanding that he enter her.

But he held her away and looked down at her with love-glazed eyes. "Silken fire and flame," he whispered. "I want to make love to you every day of my life. I want yours to be the last face I see when I close my eyes at night and the first I see when I wake in the morning. Whenever I reach my hand out to you I want you to be there for me." He smoothed the red hair away from her face. "Maybe you're right, April. Maybe I am a Latin chauvinist. And that's not going to change. I'm not going to change. Love me as I am, because you're a part of me now."

His mouth found hers again, gently, then not so gently as their passion rekindled. His hands tightened on her body as he eased himself over her, as with a groan of desire he joined his body to hers.

As they moved together, April felt the trembling of her body and of his. She felt desire and passion and a love so strong that her throat knotted with the need to cry.

"Alejandro," she whispered against his throat, "Alejandro," as she lifted her body to his in total surrender, meeting him thrust for thrust, her fingers curled in his hair, then crying out as the tempo of his desire heightened, clinging to him, whispering his name in the frenzy of the fire coursing through her body until at last, with his mouth covering hers, they reached the summit of passion and tumbled breathlessly down to the warm comfort of each others' arms, still kissing, still touching. And when he made to move away from her April whispered, "No, stay, Alejandro. Stay here inside me, my love."

Afterward, when she had fallen asleep, Alejandro continued to stroke her. And when the air grew cool he eased her off the fur spread and into bed, pulling the fur over their naked bodies.

There had been a lot of women in his life, as there were in almost every matador's life; there was a certain romantic mystique about a profession that pits man against beast that was attractive to many women.

A long time ago he had read an early theological tract that gave a description of the Devil—a large black, monstrous apparition with horns on his head, cloven hooves, hair, fiery eyes, terrible teeth and a sulfurous smell. Perhaps that definition was close to the truth, and he wondered what mystical reason drove him and so many others into the terrible danger of the bullring.

He rubbed his face against the softness of April's hair, smiling to himself in the darkness. He hadn't expected to ask her to marry him that night, but now that he had he realized it was what he wanted. He knew it wouldn't be an easy marriage, because April wasn't like any woman he had ever known. She was quicksilver and flame, fire and passion.

He smiled wryly. April would never be content to sit in the background of his life; she would always make her opinions known. And he knew deep in his soul that if he ever touched another woman, she would leave him. But he would never want another woman; he knew that as surely as he knew the sun would rise the next day.

He thought of the man April had lived with, the man who had left her, and his stomach tightened with the thought that another man had made love to her, had touched her with his hands and his body. He wished that he had been the first, but knew that he would be the last.

April stirred against him, fingers tightening on his arm as she dreamed.

"Shhh," he whispered, "shhh, my love," and felt an overwhelming tenderness. He wanted to protect her from whatever evils the world might hold—even protect her from her dreams.

April awoke before Alejandro the next morning, easing out of bed so that she wouldn't disturb him, looking at the disarray of clothes on the floor with chagrin.

The hot water of the shower felt good on her body. She scrubbed for a long time, then washed her hair. Wrapping herself in Alejandro's white terry-cloth robe, she tiptoed back into the bedroom.

Alejandro lay on his side, still asleep, the fur spread clutched to his waist as though for protection. April sat on the edge of the bed, studying his face, marveling at the long sweep of lashes, the powerful cut of his nose and jaw, the gentle curve of his mouth.

As her eyes traveled down his body, she saw again the scars that marked his bronze skin—scars from sharp horns. Then she looked up and saw the painting of the matador's wife and her breath caught in a gasp of fear, because it seemed that the dark sad eyes of the woman in the painting looked directly into hers.

And as April gazed, almost spellbound, at the woman, it seemed to her that she understood the true meaning of the painting. She wanted to weep for the woman—and for herself, because now she understood the sadness and the fear.

But as she studied the painting, she realized that the woman had something that she, April, did not have: That something was acceptance. For the woman had learned to live, day by painful day, with her fear, lighting her votive candle each time her husband fought, patient and docile as she prayed her silent prayer for his safety.

I'm not like that, April thought. I've never been patient or docile in my life. I can't change the way I am, and I can't ask Alejandro to change.

Despair filled her then, and as her gaze moved from the painting to his face, Alejandro opened his eyes. In the silence of the room they looked at each other, then he reached out and drew her to him. He didn't question the intensity of her embrace, the hunger of her mouth or the way her arms clung. He only knew that this was April and that he would never let her go.

When they left the apartment that day, he gave her a key and said, "This is your home too. Come here whenever you want to."

And when she shook her head and tried to give the key back to him, he said, "You can water my plants while I'm away."

"You don't have any plants."

"I'll buy some."

"Alejandro . . ."

But he closed her fingers around the key and said, "Keep it."

Chapter 11

AUTUMN CAME SLOWLY. ALMOST WITHOUT NOTICE THE days grew shorter and a chill in the air warned of the winter to come.

September was the time of the *vendimia*, the wine harvest, in Jerez. Every year people came from all over Europe to attend this fiesta, to see the magnificent Andalusian horses, the carriages spilling with flowers, the girls in bright dresses and the carts filled to overflowing with the lusciously ripe grapes that would be tossed to the crowds.

Wine would flow night and day and the streets would be filled with the sound of music. And in the evening *aficionados* of the flamenco would gather in their favorite clubs to sip amontillado or Manzanilla while their feet tapped to the rhythms of the guitars and the staccato beat of the dancers.

"Can you clear your desk and come with me to Jerez for the fiesta?" April asked Esteban. "I hate to pull you away, but nobody knows the operation in Jerez as well as you do. Besides, a week of good Andalusian sunshine will be good for you."

Esteban agreed, but reluctantly, it seemed to her. He asked Pepita to come with him, but she decided she would go instead to visit her mother in Cuenca and make the final preparations for the wedding.

Alejandro, who was fighting in Barcelona, planned to arrive in Jerez on Saturday and fight on Sunday. In the meantime Esteban and April would stay at La Esperanza.

The two of them left Madrid early in the morning and drove to Jaén, where they spent the night. Esteban, who had been quiet and moody all day, had more than his usual before-dinner drink and consumed a large quantity of wine with dinner. The next morning he seemed tired and out of sorts, but when April offered to drive, he told her that she was not familiar enough with his new sports car, a Fiat Spider, and that the road between Jaén and Córdoba turned and twisted, and it would be better if he drove.

He handled the small car with skill, but like all Spaniards he drove too fast, and twice April asked him to slow down when they approached a dangerous curve.

She didn't say anything when he ordered a whisky and soda at lunch. But when he signaled the waiter for a second, she said, "I'd rather you didn't, Esteban. Not if you intend to drive." And when he flashed her a glance of annoyance, she put her hand on his arm and said, "What's troubling you, *amigo?*"

"Nothing. I'm tired, that's all. Last week was hectic."

"That's not it, Esteban. I know you better than that. You've never minded hard work. What is it?"

He chewed his lower lip, darting a stubborn angry glance at her as he downed his drink. Then finally he took a deep breath and said, "It's the city, April. I hate it. I want to go back to the plant in Jerez. Or buy my own vineyard. But if I do, I know I'll lose Pepita. So what do I do? What the hell do I do?"

"Talk to her, Esteban. Tell her how you feel."

"I can't, April. I'm afraid I'll lose her. She's so excited about the wedding plans, and she's found an apartment in one of those new buildings along José Antonio. Christ, April, I don't want to live on José Antonio. The traffic and the noise would drive me crazy."

"Then you've got to tell her."

"I can't." His eyes were desperate. "I can't lose her, April. I can't."

He made the rest of the trip in moody silence. But he drove more slowly and April, though concerned about him, was able to sit back and relax.

There were so many preparations to be made for the coming fiesta: horses to be groomed, wagons to be decorated with flowers, musicians to be hired, grapes to be harvested, beautiful Andalusian girls to be gathered like roses and assigned to carriages.

April and Esteban worked long, hard hours, and although April feared that he drank too much when the day's work was done, she was glad to see that he did not touch anything while he was working.

Every evening they returned to La Esperanza. Rafa was on vacation from school and April spent as much time as she could with him. If it was still light when she returned from Jerez, she'd change her clothes and go through the fields to the small bullring to watch Rafa practice his cape work.

It was obvious, even to her untrained eye, how much he had improved since the first time she'd seen him. There was more grace to his slim body now, more skill in the movements of the cape. He liked having her watch him and told her things about the art she had not known before, like how a pass was done, what a *suerte* was, and how one bull was different from another.

And it was fun, because there was no animal in the ring with him.

On Saturday morning Esteban drove to Cádiz to meet Pepita, who arrived at eleven, and Alejandro and Carlos, who arrived an hour later.

Pepita was ebullient at dinner that night, her large brown eyes snapping with enthusiasm as she told them about the plans for the coming wedding.

"I've designed my own dress, *guapo*," she told Esteban. "It will be made of yards and yards of white lace. And I'll have a thin lace veil for my face. I'm going to wear my hair back in a coronet so that I look very ladylike and proper. You like it that way, don't you?"

"I like it any way you wear it," he said, covering her hand with his. But his eyes looked shadowed and worried, and April, glancing at him, wondered if he would tell Pepita that he couldn't live in Madrid. And if he did, what Pepita would do.

Later, when she and Alejandro were alone, she told him of her doubt.

"He's got to tell her," Alejandro said. "He can't work where he's not happy. It's up to him to tell Pepita right now that he's leaving Madrid and that they're going to live in Jerez."

"But she hates it in Jerez. She'd hate it anywhere except in Madrid."

"Esteban has to be firm. He has to show her right now that he's the boss."

April picked up a pillow off the bed and threw it at him. "Chauvinist!"

"Behave yourself, woman," he growled.

"Ha! You don't scare me." She threw the other pillow and shrieked as he came around the bed after her.

He kissed her soundly, then held her away from him and said, "I'm going to enjoy teaching you how to be a good Spanish wife, *gringa*. You'll cook my food and polish my boots and warm my bed."

"That's what you think!"

"And if you talk back to me, I'll—"

"You'll what?" April taunted.

"Do this." And before she could escape, he pulled her with him down to the bed, pulled her gown up over her head, and brought his hand down in a stinging smack across her buttocks.

"Let me up!" April cried, half angry, half amused.

"Not right away, my little pigeon. You have an extraordinarily lovely derriere, my dear Miss Juneau. Round and full. The color of pearl, except for the mark of my hand."

"Alejandro, let me up this instant or I'll—"

"You'll what?" His hand caressed her skin. "You'll what, my darling *gringa?*"

Her flesh quivered under his fingertips as he rubbed the place where he had struck her, and when she tried to move away, his hand tightened on one round cheek. "Lie still," he ordered, "or I really will paddle you."

April's breath tightened in her throat as his hand went to her thighs, lightly stroking, then returned to caress her buttocks before they crept back to the soft skin of her inner thighs.

"Alejandro . . ."

His hand warmed her, moving up and down her legs.

"Alejandro . . ." Her voice a soft moan now.

"Yes, my love? Yes, my darling?" he said as his hand

went back to her inner thighs, his fingers drifting softly and slowly between her legs as she shuddered with longing.

Finally, when she thought she could no longer bear it, he set her on her feet. Her red hair tumbled over her shoulders, her gown was in disarray. Her face was flushed.

Alejandro, his breath coming fast in his throat, said, "I'm going to love being married to you, April," and pulled her into his arms.

As her arms reached up to him, she thought, There are no problems between us that we can't solve. I'll do anything he wants me to do, be anything he wants me to be.

Then his lips were on her as his hands caressed her and he whispered words of love against her lips, making her wait while he trailed warm kisses down her throat to her peaked breasts. He held her, his hands fastened on her waist while he kissed first one, then the other, before his mouth moved down her body.

"Alejandro," April murmured, her voice thick with desire. "Alejandro, please."

"In a moment, sweet love."

She felt his breath against her skin, the singeing tingle of his lips across her belly, lingering, teasing her inner thighs before he returned to her breasts.

April fastened her hands in his thick black hair, trying to force him over her. "Please," she breathed.

"Please what?"

"You know."

"Tell me."

"Come up over me. I want to feel the weight of you on me."

His tongue flicked a breast. "Is that all?"

"Alec, darling . . ."

"What else, April?"

"Inside me," she whispered.

"Tell me!" His hands tightened around her waist. "Tell me, love."

"Inside me," she cried. "Oh, Alec, Alec."

He came up over her and kissed her mouth. "Yes, my darling," he said against her lips. And with a low groan of need he entered her.

Gently but forcefully, lovingly demanding, his body claimed her, and with each powerful thrust he seemed to say, "You're mine. Mine. Mine."

April's arms encircled his back; her fingers stroked his smooth bronze skin; her body lifted to his in a hunger that matched his own and made him shudder with pleasure. She tasted the skin of his shoulder, nipping it in her excitement, urging him closer, her hands at the small of his back to press him to her as she raised her body to his. Then, reaching for his thick black hair, she brought his mouth down to hers, caressing the inside of his lips with her tongue, whimpering in ecstasy when he caught her lower lip between his teeth to suck it the way he would a ripe plum. And all the while her body was frantic with desire as she moved with complete abandon under his strong body.

Until it was past bearing. Until she cried his name and felt his hands tighten on her body as together they tumbled over the peak of desire to the safe warmth of each other's arms.

He was gone before April awoke on Sunday morning. She knew that he was at the *sorteo* with Carlos and that she would not see him until after the day's bullfight.

She lay for a long time, watching the sun streaming in

through the wide windows, her body pleasantly tired from a night of love. She knew there were things to do, that she should get up and bathe and perhaps do an hour or two of work at the office. But it was Sunday and all she wanted to do at the moment was lie here and think about Alejandro.

She really had not known what it was to love a man so completely, to love being with him, to feel incomplete without him, to hold back nothing. Making love to Alejandro was exciting and wondrous, but there was more to it than that. It was lying beside him when he slept, reaching out in the night and knowing he was next to her, falling asleep in his arms and feeling him curled against her back at night.

It would not be an easy marriage. They were different people, from very different cultures. Alejandro had not been joking when he said that there were no equal partners in a marriage, that he would be the head of the family, which was just a nice way of saying he'd be the boss.

Perhaps he'd soften in time. Perhaps she could love some of that Spanish machismo out of him. And while she intended to be a good wife, she would always be her own woman. Nothing could change that.

But it was not the problem of his chauvinism or her American independence that worried April. She could cope with those things and hopefully, with grace and humor, overcome his prejudices. But she was not sure she could cope with his profession for another eight or nine years or even another eight or nine *corridas*. How many times could she watch him take chances with his life? How long could she hide her fear from him?

Then, because she wanted to be alone, she had breakfast in her room and went over the final arrangements for the harvest festival. When it was time to get ready, she showered and dressed in a tan suede skirt and blouson jacket, a sheer bronze-tone blouse and matching high-heeled pumps and bag. After she had brushed her auburn hair back from her face and snapped her amber earrings on, she leaned her hands on the edge of the dressing table and, half afraid to meet her own eyes in the mirror, whispered, "I won't be afraid this time. I won't!"

But she was. The minute Alejandro stepped out to meet his first bull, her stomach tightened with fear. But she raged inwardly, because Carlos was sitting beside her.

"I think I'll watch from the *barrera* today," he'd told Alejandro. "It will be exciting for Rafa to be in the *callejón* with you. Let him be your sword boy."

The magenta and yellow cape in his hands, Alejandro called the bull to him in an opening *verónica*, another and another as the bull charged, ending with a *media-verónica*, the horns passing close to his legs, so close that April winced.

When it was time for the *banderillas*, he did them himself, spinning away from the horns each time with only a fraction of an inch to spare.

Then the final *tercio*. When Rafa handed him the semifolded *muleta*, he took it in his left hand, then the sword in his right, and came to stand under their *barrera* to dedicate the *faena*.

"To the engaged couple," he said. "I wish you love." Then, with a smile at April, he turned his back and tossed his black *montera* to Esteban, and the last *tercio* began.

Carlos hunched forward in his seat, his eyes on Alejandro, murmuring under his breath, "That's it. Yes, yes, careful now. Closer. No, damnit, not that close. A *natural*. That's it. Again. Yes, beautiful, most beautiful."

"That's a magnificent animal," Esteban said.

"And a magnificent matador fighting him," Carlos added. "Can you imagine a mediocre matador with that bull? The Miuras are the largest, the most treacherous animals in the world."

"Wasn't it a Miura that killed Manolete?" Pepita asked nervously.

Carlos nodded. "But it wouldn't have killed him if he hadn't been so damned honest. He knew the bull, Islero, had a tendency to lean to the right. He could have gone in over the center when he made the kill. But he refused to compensate, to cheat just a little. He went to the right and the bull killed him."

And April, listening, thought, I hate this. Oh, God, how I hate this. She pressed her nails in her palms, listening in anger, when Pepita squealed with excitement and Esteban shouted, *"Olé! Olé, Alec!"*

A *trincherazo* with the *muleta* and sword held low in his right hand over his left thigh. A *manoletina,* looking into the stands rather than at the bull when the animal charged. Pass after pass, closer and still closer. Then a perfect *remate* with a small whip of the *muleta* before he turned away from the bull.

Excitement mounted as the band played a *diana* and the crowd shouted their approval.

"The knowledgeable fans know the great merit in fighting a bull like that is that every movement has to be sure and steady," Carlos said. "Miuras have a sixth sense. They feel any doubt or hesitation on the part of the *matador*. Notice that Alejandro doesn't move an inch backward. No matter how close the bull is to his body, he holds his ground. This is a fantastic *faena*, Esteban. Fantastic!"

Sweat beaded April's upper lip.

Alejandro knelt in front of the bull. He reached to touch the horns. Then slowly he turned his back on the animal.

The bitter taste of fear rose in her throat as the seconds passed.

The crowd, which had been holding its collective breath, burst into wild applause as Alejandro stood and touched the bull's head.

"Excuse me."

"What's the matter?" Esteban asked. "Where are you going?"

"Just to get a glass of water. I've got a headache. I want to take a couple of aspirin."

"I'll get it for you."

She swallowed hard. "No, no, that's all right," she said, pushing past him, shaking her head when Pepita offered to go with her, trying not to run as she made her way up toward the exit.

The stairs tilted. She reached for the railing to keep from falling as her knees buckled.

Suddenly a hand was on her arm. A voice said, "Steady. Over this way," and she was led behind the stands.

An arm supported her shoulders; another around her back held her at the waist so that she wouldn't fall when she retched. Too weak to protest, April leaned against the arms that supported her and accepted a clean white handkerchief when her stomach was empty.

Only when she straightened did she see that the man who had helped her was Carlos Manzanares.

Without speaking, he led her to a stone bench, and when she sat down he said, "Close your eyes and lean back. A few deep breaths will help."

April did as he told her, shame and embarrassment coursing through her, because this man who disliked her so much had seen her this way.

"I'm sorry," she managed to say after a few minutes. "It was probably something I ate for breakfast."

"No, it was not something you ate, Señorita Juneau. Do not lie to me and, more importantly, do not lie to yourself."

April's back stiffened and in a cold, hollow voice she said, "I don't know what you mean."

"I mean that you are terrified."

"No!"

"You are sick with terror." He took a deep breath. "As I am, Señorita Juneau. As I am."

April gasped in surprise as she stared at him.

But before she could speak, he said, "We cannot help ourselves because we both love Alec. To me he is the son I never had. To you? I am not quite sure."

"I'm going to marry him."

"Yes, I was afraid of that."

"Because you don't like me."

"Because you will change him."

"No. No, I'd never do that."

"You won't be able to help yourself. You should have seen the way you looked a few minutes ago. White, shaking, ready to fly into a million pieces. How long do you think you can hide this from Alec? How long before your fear makes him afraid?"

A part of April knew that he was right. But she would not admit it, could not admit it. So, with her chin high, with defiance in her eyes, she said, "I'm going to marry Alec. But he will continue to be his own man, just as I will continue to be my own woman."

Manzanares smiled. "You American women," he

said, but not unkindly. "You're going to lead poor Alec on a merry chase. I hope you won't be too much of a shock for that Latin blood of his. But then, there is nothing a Spaniard loves better than a challenge. It's going to be an interesting marriage."

He held out his hand. "We might as well be friends, Señorita Juneau. I have a feeling you're going to be with us for a very long time."

"What happened to you and Carlos?" Alejandro asked her later. "I looked up and you weren't there."

"I had a headache. I went to find a glass of water and Carlos went with me."

He looked at her strangely. "Are you sure that's all it was, April?"

"I—I don't know what you mean, Alec."

"Did you have a headache when I fought in Valencia? You left the ring that day too."

"Yes, but—"

He put a finger under her chin and forced her to look at him. "Don't lie to me, April. I can stand anything but that. Did you leave the ring because you were afraid?"

"Of course not!" She turned away from him and in an almost angry voice said, "You know I like bullfights. I love the color and the pageantry and the—the excitement."

"It's not different for you when I'm in the ring?"

"Well, darling . . ." She summoned what she hoped was a bright smile and said, "Of course the excitement is sharper when it's you. And that's not just because I'm in love with you, Señor Cervantes. It's because you're better than anybody else."

Then another small lie: "I waited until you killed the first bull before I went out for the aspirin." She touched his face lightly with her fingertips. "Besides, it was your fault I had a headache. You really didn't let me get much sleep last night."

Then, as she had planned he would, he pulled her into his arms. And he did not ask her again why she had left the *corrida*.

Chapter 12

"WHAT IN THE WORLD IS THE MATTER WITH YOU?" APRIL spoke impatiently as she frowned at her secretary across the desk. "All you've done this last week is scowl at me and everybody else. What's bothering you?"

"Nothing."

"Come on, Pepita, let's get it out in the open. Are you angry with me for some reason? Have I done something to offend you?"

"No, it's not you, April. It's Esteban." Her dark eyes flashed with anger. "He says he doesn't want to live in Madrid."

"I'm sorry, Pepita. But if he isn't happy here . . ."

"He would be if he'd just give it a chance." Her forehead puckered in a frown. "You can make him stay, April. You could talk to Señor Alvarez and have him tell Esteban that, as far as his job is concerned, it's Madrid or nothing." Her eyes were pleading, her voice plaintive. "Please, April. You can do it."

"No, I can't. But even if I could, Pepita, I wouldn't. Esteban has to make his own decisions."

"Even if it means I'm going to be miserable for the rest of my life?"

"But if you love Esteban, what difference does it make where you live as long as you're with him?"

"It makes a lot of difference to me."

"Look, dear, I know Jerez isn't Madrid, but it's a nice place. You'd be near Seville and Cádiz. Close to Tangier. It's a marvelous location."

"Not for me! Oh, I'm so unhappy I could die." She leaned her head on the desk and began to cry.

April, biting her lip, wondering what she could say to make Pepita feel better, came swiftly around the desk and put her arms around the sobbing girl. "Talk to Esteban, Pep. Maybe you can compromise, work something out so that he can spend the summers at the vineyard in Jerez and the winters here. He'll have to give up the foreign sales job, but maybe something can be arranged."

Pepita sat up and wiped her eyes. "He's coming back at the end of the week," she sniffed. "He said we'd talk then. It's not just that he wants to leave Madrid, April. He's talking about leaving the company, about buying his own vineyard. *Dios mío!* I'd be right back where I was when I was a girl, grubbing in the dirt for a living."

"You wouldn't be grubbing," April said with a smile. "Not with Esteban." Then, in a more serious tone, she said, "Do you love him, Pepita?"

"Of course I love him." She wiped her eyes. "But I love Madrid too. I love the way of life we could have here—the apartment I picked out and the furniture. It's all g-g-glass and chrome and it's just—just beautiful."

"You can still use it in Jerez—or anywhere else, for that matter."

"But I don't want it anywhere else." Pepita's face,

now that she had composed herself, was stiff and closed.

April, although she sympathized with Pepita, could not help feeling a little annoyed. If the girl really loved Esteban, she'd live wherever he wanted to. He couldn't help being the kind of a man he was. He loved farming and he loved the land. But he loved Pepita too and he'd make a good life for her.

Well, perhaps there were always things about a man that most women would change if given the opportunity, April thought. Certainly she didn't like the fact that Alejandro was a matador, but because that was what he did, she accepted it.

That wasn't a fair comparison, of course. All Esteban wanted to do was grow grapes. That was very different from risking your life in a bullring.

During the next week April gave herself several talkings-to. Alejandro had two fights scheduled in Guadalajara on the weekend. She would go and she would *not* behave like a fool. She'd enjoy the spectacle if it killed her.

She was still determinedly cheerful on Saturday morning when Alejandro asked her if she wanted to go to the *sorteo* with him. After breakfast they met Carlos, and the three of them went to the bullring for the drawing of the bulls the matadors would fight that afternoon. Although April gasped when she saw the size of the animals, she managed to hide how she felt and to show an interest when each matador drew the paper balls with the numbers of the bulls from the proffered hat.

"I don't like your second one," Carlos said to Alejandro. "There's something wrong with his left eye. His line of vision seems faulty. You'll have to remember to compensate."

"I'll remember. He's got good lines."

"But uneven horns. I wish you hadn't drawn him."

"We've had worse," Alejandro said with a touch of arrogance. "The day has not yet arrived when I can't handle an animal like him."

Later, when they were having an aperitif, April sat next to Carlos and asked, "Why is it so bad if there's something wrong with one of the eyes?"

He hesitated, then, with a serious look, said, "If a bull is blind in one eye, he'll charge like he's crashing into a car. Also, like a person who is blind, his hearing and other instincts are sharper. If he feels even the slightest movement or a presence on that side, he's very likely to slash out with his horns. A *matador* has to learn to recognize imperfections and compensate for them. I was only cautioning Alec, April. He knows how to handle that kind of a bull." He studied her face a moment and, lowering his voice, said, "Why don't you say you're tired and stay at the hotel this afternoon?"

She shook her head. "No, Carlos. And I promise you, I'm not going to get sick again. I'm going to sit there and smile and—"

"Tell him how you feel, April."

She looked at him. Slowly she shook her head. "I can't," she said. "I can't."

The bull with the bad eye caught Alejandro at the beginning of the *faena;* caught him, slammed him to the earth and, with horns slashing, attacked.

But miraculously the horns didn't catch Alejandro. When his *cuadrilla* lured the bull away, Alejandro jumped to his feet and, waving them out of the ring, called the bull to him again.

He began with an *ayudado por alto*, holding the *muleta* in his left hand, spread by the sword that he held

in his right, provoking the charge as he remained quite
still until just before the bull lowered its head. Then,
with his feet firm on the sand, he moved his hands
slightly out, away from his body, raising the *muleta* with
a twist of his wrists so that the bull thundered by him.
As the animal turned, Alejandro repeated the pass.

There was an electric current of excitement in the air
now. The bull had had his taste of blood, and he
wanted to catch the red cape and the man behind it.
And Alejandro, angry because he'd been tossed, was
determined to master the bull.

With delicate continuity he began a series of *naturales,* citing the animal sideways to offer the cape. When
the bull charged, Alejandro stood as though rooted to
the spot and moved the cloth in a smooth swinging arc,
weaving the long, viciously pointed horns around and
past his body as the crowd jumped to their feet to
scream their approval.

He was the ultimate matador now: eyes, chin, chest
all in a line, following the cloth, his body twisting from
the waist as he led the bull. And when the bull was past,
he stood slim and straight, head thrown back, hands on
his hips. Arrogantly handsome. The perfect male.

Behind her April heard a woman say, *"Por Dios!* I
would give a year of my life to go to bed with that
man."

Now he did a *trincherazo* to the left side, then the
right. A *pase del desdén* that brought the crowd to their
feet. A series of *manoletinas* and the flashy *afarolado,*
passing the bull to his side, whirling the *muleta* over his
head as the horns swept by his body.

The crowd went wild. Calls of *"Torero, Torero,"*
filled the bullring, and the woman behind April chant-
ed, "Al-e-jan-dro! Al-e-jan-dro!"

On the sand below, the man and the bull faced each

other as Alejandro dropped to his knees, *muleta* and sword behind him, his face only inches away from the bull's.

April, watching him, was suddenly so angry that she forgot to be ill—too angry even to join in the adulation that followed the final sword. When he received his award of two ears and made his triumphant tour of the ring, she didn't stand up and cheer as the others did. She sat right where she was and glared at him.

The woman behind her sailed a black patent high-heeled sandal over April's head. Alejandro picked it up, touched it to his lips and, with a smile, tossed it back to the ecstatic woman.

He drank from the *botas* of wine that were tossed, accepted the flowers with dignified grace and finally walked to the center of the ring, where he bowed, hands across his chest in a gesture that showed he embraced them all.

"Magnificent!" the woman behind April said to her companion. "I've never seen anything like him."

"Neither have I!" April muttered to herself. "Neither have I."

When they were alone in her room that night, April, looking at Alejandro as though she wished she had a cape and a sword in her hands, said, "Did you have to be so damned macho today?"

"What?" He seemed genuinely surprised. "What are you talking about?"

"I'm talking about your performance this afternoon. You were so—so arrogant! So sure of yourself. You dared the bull to hook you. And you strutted like a damned peacock. *Dios!* I thought the woman in back of me was going to leap over the *barrera* and attack you!"

His grin was wicked. "You're jealous."

"I'm *not* jealous." She wanted to shake him. "I don't give a damn about those silly women who scream and shout their silly *olé*'s. You're a hero figure and I understand that. But I don't understand why you take idiotic and inexcusable chances with your life."

"I don't take idiotic chances." He glared at her and then, in what April thought was a supercilious voice, said, "You don't know anything about this, April. You don't understand the profession, so don't try to tell me how to fight."

"I'm not trying to tell you how to fight. But I darn well refuse to sit there and watch you try to kill yourself."

"I'm not trying to kill myself. I know what I'm doing."

"Did you know what you were doing when the bull caught your leg a month ago?"

"That was an accident."

"And all the other times?"

When he refused to meet her eyes, she said, "I've seen the scars, Alejandro, so I know how many times the bulls have caught you. I know how many wounds you have."

"Wounds are a part of the profession. There can be accidents in any profession, April."

"Any profession?" Hands on her hips, she glared at him. "Like what?"

"Like house-painting." He grinned at her.

She was so stunned, she could only stare at him.

"A house painter can fall off a ladder. An archaeologist can have a dig fall in on him. A bookkeeper can stab himself with his pencil."

"You're impossible!"

"And you're unreasonable. If you don't like watching me fight, then stay away from the bullring."

"And do what? Sit at home like that woman in the painting and mend your jacket? I'm not like that, Alejandro, I'll never be like that."

"That, my dear, is quite obvious. A Spanish woman has enough sense to stay home while her man is fighting. And she doesn't interfere in something she doesn't understand."

"Oh, I understand all right," April said, stung by his words. "I understand your need to prove how macho you are, your need to strut and—"

He grabbed her arms and shook her. "Damnit, that's enough!"

"How long are you going to do it, Alejandro? Are you going to fight until a bull kills you or hurts you so badly you'll never fight again? Do you want to end up like Rufino Briviesca? Alone and minus a leg?"

"Alone?" Alejandro's face was white. "What in the hell is that supposed to mean?"

"Nothing." April bit her lip, afraid for a moment that she'd gone too far.

"You're not by any chance threatening me, are you, April?" His hands held her in a viselike grip. Even when she winced he did not release her. "Are you, April?" he said again.

"No." Her voice was so low he could barely hear her.

She hated herself for backing down, but something made her stop. A part of her mind whispered, "If you go on now, there will be no turning back. You don't want to lose him, do you?"

No, she thought. I don't want to lose him. But how can I bear to live with the kind of fear I felt this afternoon?

Alejandro had told her that he planned to keep on fighting for eight or nine more years. How could she continue to watch his terrible dance with death Sunday after Sunday? How could she live with that kind of fear?

If he really loved her, he wouldn't put her through that kind of agony. If he knew how she suffered whenever he was in the ring . . .

Thoughts skittered in April's head. Then she focused on one single thought: If Alejandro loves you, you can make him quit.

Lifting her face, she looked into his green Gypsy eyes and whispered, "I'm sorry, Alejandro. Don't be angry, darling. I guess I'm just a *gringa* and I'm—I'm so terribly in love with you that the thought of your being . . . of your being hurt terrifies me."

She began to unbutton his shirt. "No more scenes, Alec. I promise." She nuzzled her face against his bare chest while her hands reached to pull the shirt away from his trousers so that she could slip her hands around his back.

"No scenes—unless one of those female fans of yours tries to take you away from me." She nipped his shoulder, then soothed it with her tongue, and all the while her fingers played against the smoothness of his back. "I could've killed the woman sitting behind me today when she kept shouting your name." She tickled his chest with dozens of kisses and nibbles.

When she heard the hiss of his breath in his throat, she reached around to unfasten his belt and slipped her hands lower on his back as she urged him gently toward her until the long length of his body was against hers.

When his breath quickened, she stepped away from him and, taking his hand, led him to the bed and pushed him back against the pillows. Then, with hands that trembled and lingered, she began slowly to undress him, stopping now and then to gaze into his eyes, to touch him with her lips.

When he lay naked and waiting, his eyes narrowed with desire, April dimmed the light and, turning away from him, slipped out of her clothes, then reached into the closet for the pink gown that he had given her.

She could feel his eyes on her as she went to the dresser, making herself go slowly now in spite of the flame that kindled and grew within her. She began to brush her hair, deliberately taking her time, letting the strokes run from her high forehead down to below her shoulders, brushing until her hair shone like dark fire in the dim light of the room. Next, with agonizing slowness, she dabbed perfume on her temples and throat and between her breasts.

"Come here," Alejandro said in a voice that was hoarse with need.

A pulse drummed in April's throat as she turned to look at him.

He lay prone, his naked body dark against the whiteness of the sheet, green eyes ablaze with desire, nostrils flared, lips drawn back from his white teeth in angry need.

Slowly, April let her eyes travel down the length of his body, drinking in the sight of his broad, muscular shoulders, the wide chest covered with curling black hair, the narrow waist and hips, the long, perfect legs.

"April!"

She stood, stretched a lazy cat stretch and moved silently across the room toward him. When she reached the bed, she sat on the edge. She put a finger against his lips, then ever so slowly let it travel down his body.

His hand reached out to stop her. "Enough!" he said in an angry voice. "Enough!" Then he pulled her down beside him. His mouth was on hers and he kissed her as though he were consuming her, his mouth possessively cruel as he whispered her name and tightened his hands on her body.

"No," April whispered against his lips.

Startled, he let her go, and she leaned over him, her red hair falling across his chest, and said, "I want to make love to you tonight."

He tried to speak, but she covered his mouth with kisses, willing him to respond to her softness, to the slow warmth of her tongue exploring the recesses of his mouth. Tenderly she pressed moist kisses along his earlobes before she moved down to his throat and chest, trailing her fiery hair across his body as she kissed him, as her hands caressed him, feeling a thrill of passion when he gasped with desire, retreating when he reached for her.

"You make me wait," she whispered. "Tonight you must wait."

"Witch. My *gringa* witch." His fingers entwined in the thickness of her hair as he brought her face down to his. "I want you now."

"In a minute, love." She nipped his ear gently. "That's what you tell me, isn't it? When I'm longing to have you over me? When my body lifts to yours? When I beg you to make love to me?"

She ran a finger across his lips. "You make me wait, darling."

"Because I love to have you tell me what you want."

"I know." Her body moved against his. "I know, my love."

"*Dios*, April, no more! No more!" He pulled her to him, forcing her onto her back as he pulled the pink cloud of gown aside and came up over her. He looked down into her eyes and whispered her name, half in love, half in anger. Then, grasping her hips, he joined his body to hers.

She cried out with the sheer joy of having him inside her at last and heard him growl his need as he pulled her closer. Now they were truly one, moving as one entity in the perfect rhythm of love.

Alejandro's mouth sought and found hers, and his arms pulled her closer. Closer. Until April was swept away in a mad whirl of emotions, of love and want and need and a keen desire that carried her to a plateau that was half agony and half ecstasy.

"Alejandro," she whispered in sweet anguish, "Alejandro."

Then, in a wild burst of joy that was past bearing, she clung to him and whispered his name and told him of her love.

It was only afterward, when he stroked her to calmness, that she remembered she had planned this, that she had wanted to show Alejandro how much she loved him and make his need so great that he would never let her go.

But the next morning, as she looked at his scars while she watched him dress, her resolve of the night before strengthened.

When he was dressed he came to sit beside her on the bed. He leaned down and kissed her and said, "You're a strange and wonderful woman, April. Sometimes you look as though you belong in a church, saying your beads. At other times you're the very essence of what a sophisticated woman of the world should be, every inch a lady." He smoothed the tumbled hair back from her face. "And last night you were the perfect courtesan. I felt as though I'd never get enough of you."

"I know I'll never get enough of you, Alejandro." She entwined her fingers with his. "I'm sorry I quarreled with you last night. But I—I love you so much, darling." She rubbed the back of his hand against her face. "I lied when I said I wasn't afraid, Alec. I am afraid. So afraid that I die a little every time you step into the ring."

"April—"

"Yesterday, when you were so close to the bull, when his horns were only inches away from your face . . ." She closed her eyes, unable to go on.

"It's my profession, April. It's what I do." His voice was strained.

"I know, darling. I don't want to change you." She reached up and touched his face. "But if you could be—if you could just not take such terrible chances. You're at the height of your career. You don't have to prove anything to anybody. You could . . . hold back a little."

His dark brows came together in a scowl.

"Just give a little less, Alec," she said in a pleading voice. "Don't do the dangerous passes. The crowd will still like you. Most of them won't know the difference."

"I can't do that!"

She could feel the tears form. "Not even for me?" she whispered. "Not even when you know that I'm sick with terror?"

"April . . ." His face was white.

"Oh, Alejandro. Alejandro, I love you so." Then she was in his arms, sobbing as though her heart would break.

His body was stiff against hers. Then she felt him sigh as his arms went around her, and she knew that she had won.

Chapter 13

ALEJANDRO BEGAN THE *FAENA* WITH MORE CAUTION THAN usual, telling himself that his was a dangerous animal and that it was best to go slowly at first. He did a *pase de la muerte,* a pass of death, with his arms extended a little more than usual. He cited the bull with the *muleta,* then flexed his wrists to lift the cloth when the bull charged.

Next he did a series of *naturales,* facing the bull, the sword in his right hand behind his back as he offered the *muleta* with his left hand. When the bull approached, he swayed with the attack and moved the red cloth in a slow swing ahead of the bull, pulling the animal ahead of his body. He ended the series with a chest pass and won a round of applause.

Alejandro relaxed. It was all right, he thought, the crowd was with him. Perhaps April was right: Perhaps he should go a bit easier, take fewer chances. What, after all, did the crowd know? What did he owe them?

Alejandro held the sword and red cape in his right hand while he gripped a corner of the cloth behind his back with his left hand. When the bull charged, he turned to lift the red cloth to pass the horns by his body and under his arm. When the horns swept past him, he turned his body to meet the bull again, almost completing a circle. He had seen matadors cheat with the *manoletina* by taking a step along the passing flank, to walk away from the horns instead of standing still. But he had never done the pass that way. Until now.

The crowd protested when he positioned the bull for the kill. Sometimes when they did that he'd smile up into the stands and execute a few more passes or *adornos*. But today he didn't. He lined the bull up and quickly and cleanly went in over the horns.

The applause was perfunctory. When he stepped behind the *barrera* he took a scoop of water and rinsed his mouth, trying not to look at Carlos. But finally of course he had to look at the man who had been his friend all these years.

The dark eyes questioned but did not judge.

"I—I didn't like him," Alejandro found himself saying. "There was something wrong with his right eye. I didn't want to take any chances."

"Of course not. You'll have better luck with the next one."

But he wouldn't have been able to do anything with the second bull even if he'd wanted to, because the animal was a *manso*, a coward who refused to charge the horses and pawed the earth as he looked for a way out of the ring. And so Alejandro told himself there was nothing to be done with this animal, and after a few passes he dispatched him.

Still Carlos said nothing. They drove back to the hotel and only then did Carlos say, "Why don't we all have a drink together after you change? Is April leaving tonight or in the morning?"

"Early in the morning," Alejandro answered without looking at his manager.

"Well, then I'm sure the two of you would like to be alone this evening. But let's meet in the bar before you go to dinner."

"Fine."

But Alejandro didn't meet them. He went to a cafe where he sat in one of the booths and drank alone. When he left the bar, he walked for a long time without any sense of direction. He thought about his career, and he thought about April and what she meant to him. He did not think that he wanted to live his life without her, but he knew he could not live the way she wanted him to.

Finally, because he knew that he had to face her, he returned to the hotel. When he knocked at her door, she opened it, looking at him with an expression of both worry and anger.

"Where in the world have you been?" she asked when he went into the room. "Carlos and I waited and waited for you."

"Did you eat?"

"Yes, we ate here at the hotel." Her voice was impatient. "Alejandro, what is it? Where have you been? Why did you just disappear?"

"Because I had to be alone for a while, April." He saw the fear in her face then and, in a gentle voice, said, "Let's sit down. I want to talk to you."

She swallowed, nibbling her bottom lip as she looked at him. Then, pulling her robe close around her as though to protect herself, she went to sit in one of the chairs by the window.

But he didn't sit across from her as she expected. Instead he paced up and down the length of the room before he finally stopped beside her chair. He looked down at her. Then, taking a deep breath he said, "Today I cheated on a performance. I have never done that before and I will never do it again."

"But . . ."

He held up his hand. "Hear me out," he said. "From the day I first stepped into a ring, I have been totally honest in what I've done. The great *matadors,* men like Arruza, Gaona, Belmonte and Manolete, were honest men who always performed to the very best of their abilities."

"And it killed Manolete," April said in a stiff voice.

"April . . ." His eyes were concerned as he wondered how he could make her understand. He saw her pain and her fear, but he did not know how to help her.

"I'll never be as great as they were, April. But I have to be as good as *I* can be. Everybody has to do what they can to the best of their ability."

He knelt beside her and took her cold hands in his. "Don't you see that asking somebody to be less than they are is to diminish them? If Pavarotti did not hit the notes that he knew he could hit, if Baryshnikov did not extend himself to those beautifully impossible limits, neither man would be true to his art. He would be less than he could be."

He put his hand on the side of her face. "I love you, April," he said. "I want to marry you and spend my life with you. But I can't change. Not even for you."

The room was silent. Alejandro saw her throat work with the need to cry.

"I'm sorry," she whispered.

"April . . ."

She shook her head. "I can't, Alejandro. I can't marry you because I don't think I can live with the kind of fear I feel when you're in the ring. If you leave the profession . . ."

He let go of her hands and stood up. Slowly he shook his head. "I can't do that, April. I won't allow you to put conditions on our love."

"It's not a condition," she protested, angry now. "If you love me—" Then she stopped, biting back the words. "I'm sorry," she said again. "I'm sorry that this is where it ends."

"So am I, April." He saw the pain in her eyes and he wanted to gather her in his arms and tell her that he would be whatever she wanted him to be. But he knew that he could not and he did not touch her, because he knew that if he did, he would be lost.

Instead he said, "You're leaving in the morning?"

"Yes. I want to be in Madrid by nine."

"Drive carefully."

"I will."

"Good-bye, April."

"Good-bye, Alejandro."

When she closed the door he stood there for several minutes, waiting, willing her to open it, to call him back. But the door remained closed and finally he turned away and went down the long, lonely corridor to his own room.

Chapter 14

FOR APRIL THE DAYS OF AUTUMN PASSED WITH AGONIZING slowness. October was a sad month, she thought, for it was an ending—an ending of summer sun and summer flowers, of summer smells and summer promises. It was a harbinger of cold winds, gray skies and the bleakness of winter.

She tried to lose herself in work; often she skipped lunch and worked long beyond dinnertime. She grew thin and pale and knew when she looked in the mirror that her face was pinched and that there was a tightness to her mouth that had not been there before.

Each Monday morning she read the newspaper to see what had happened at Sunday's *corridas*. Alejandro fought in Albacete, Salamanca, Zamora and Valladolid. The week before he'd been in Lisbon but had returned to appear in a festival in Barcelona.

He had not tried to contact her.

It was better this way, April told herself. Alejandro could not help the way he was and she could not help the way she felt. They had been right to make a clean break. But knowing they had been right did not stop the pain of missing him.

Now, in a strange way, she understood how Pepita had felt when she told Esteban that she wouldn't live in Jerez. They'd both given their men ultimatums. She had lost but Pepita still had a chance to get what she wanted. Esteban had returned to Madrid and had agreed to give the vice-presidency another try.

Each day Pepita grew more sure of herself and of Esteban. She looked radiant in her new clothes of bright red, orange, yellow and vivid green, clothes that she wore with a flair that made other women pale by comparison. With her black-velvet hair curling about her face, dark eyes and long lashes, her cherry-red lips full and pouting, there was an untamed Gypsy look about her that made men turn and gape, their eyes wide with frank appreciation.

But it was obvious to anyone who saw them together that Pepita was in love with Esteban and that he was the only man in her life, and it was obvious that he adored her. As she moved through the office, short skirts swirling about her shapely legs, his eyes followed her. Often April had to look away, feeling a surge of sympathy at the naked love in Esteban's eyes.

Was it good to love someone that much? she wondered. Was it wise to show how much you truly cared about another person? She worried, because even though Esteban was in love with Pepita, he did not appear to be happy.

"What is it?" she asked him one day when they were alone in his office, going over figures of the next year's anticipated production. "You look almost as unhappy as I feel."

"You still haven't heard from Alec?"

April shook her head. "No. I don't suppose I will; he was very final when he left. He'll never change, Esteban. He's going to keep fighting for years. And I can't—I can't live with that."

"But you love him."

"Oh, yes, I love him. I love him so much that sometimes I want to throw everything aside and run to him." She took a deep breath. "But I won't. I won't."

"Poor April."

She tried to smile. "That's right. Poor me. Now what about you? Is the work getting any better?"

He shook his head. "It never will, April. I don't belong here. I know it, you know it, even Alvarez knows it. The land is the only place I can really be myself, the only place I can breathe." He put his head in his hands and, in a muffled voice, said, "But I can't lose Pepita, April. I don't think I could go on without her."

"What about the plans you had for your own vineyard?"

"I have the land. You see, I thought that maybe some day Pepita would change her mind. It's a beautiful place, about fifty miles from Jerez. Right on the Guadalquivir River. There are trees and a house, which needs a lot of work. But I thought that the two of us . . ." He shook his head. "I guess I'm dreaming, April. I don't think anything in this world will change Pepita's mind about farming."

"Perhaps in time she'll come around." But even as April said the words, she knew they were not true. She wished she knew some way to help them, but if she could not help herself, how could she help anyone else?

Now, as Esteban rearranged the papers on his desk, he said, "I almost forgot to tell you: Rafa's making his debut next Sunday."

April stared at him. "Rafa? But he's only a boy."

"He'll be fifteen next month, April. If he's going to have a career as a *matador,* this is the time to start."

"How can Alejandro allow . . . ?"

"Alejandro and I come from a ranching family. We've grown up with the bulls. My grandfather owned a brave-bull ranch. My father was a *matador.* Rafa's older brother tried to be a *novillero* a few years ago, but he didn't have the heart for it. I think Rafa does. Alec thinks so too."

"And he wants Rafa to be just like him, I suppose." There was a touch of bitterness in her voice.

"That's not it, April. Rafa is good. He'll be as good as Alec some day. If he's determined to fight, then he's lucky to have someone like Alec to help him."

"I suppose you're right," she said, even though she didn't think he was. And she tried to tuck the thought of Rafa away, just as she tried to hide all her thoughts of Alejandro.

But on Thursday of that week Rafa telephoned.

"Señorita Juneau? April?"

For a moment she didn't recognize his voice.

"Yes?"

"This is Rafael. Rafael Hernandez."

"Rafa? How nice to hear your voice. How are you?"

"*Muy bien.*" She heard him clear his throat. "Ah, April, did you know that I'm—that I'm going to make my debut as a *novillero* next Sunday?"

"Yes, dear. Esteban told me."

"In Segovia."

"That's wonderful, Rafa. If . . . if it's what you want."

"It's what I want." He cleared his throat again. "April, Segovia isn't too far from Madrid. I was wondering if . . . if maybe you could come. I mean come and watch me."

"Well, I—I don't know, Rafa."

"I've already reserved tickets for you. And for Esteban and Pepita. I thought maybe you could all drive together. I'd really like to see you."

She bit her lip, thinking of all the reasons why she shouldn't go. The biggest reason, of course, was that she would have to see Alejandro.

Then she thought of Rafa and of how he felt about his debut, of how important it was to him, and she said, "Of course I'll come, Rafa. I wouldn't miss it for anything in the world. I'll be there and I'll be the one shouting the loudest *olé*'s."

She could hear his pleased laugh and the relief in his voice when he said, "Uncle Alec will make your hotel reservations and everything. My brother Manuel is coming. And my grandmother. We're all going out to dinner Saturday night."

"Well, then, it's going to be an exciting weekend, isn't it? I can hardly wait to see you, Rafa. I've missed you."

"Me, too, April. See you Saturday. Okay?"

"Okay."

She smiled as she hung up the phone. It was true, she really had missed him. She liked Rafa, and if she ever had a son, she hoped he would have Rafa's qualities. After all, she was going to see *him*—just him.

But, just in case, she bought a new dress for Saturday night. "Anything except pink," she told the salesgirl, who frowned and said, "But with your coloring, *señorita*—"

"Anything but pink," April said again.

The dress she selected was a white wool with a softly

rolled collar, long sleeves and a slim, straight skirt. With it she wore a long caramel-colored Spanish vest that cost a month's pay. She pulled her hair back off her face in a sleek chignon and knew she looked elegant.

But she didn't feel sophisticated when she walked into the Mesón de Candido, an old Spanish inn that stood in the shadow of the aqueduct, and was shown to a private dining room filled with people she had never seen before.

Alejandro, dressed in a dark tailored suit, came to meet her when she entered with Esteban and Pepita. His face looked strained and tired as he took her hand and in a formal voice said, "I'm glad you could come."

April nodded, unable for a moment to speak, feeling awkward and strange, not sure whether she wanted to run away or throw herself into his arms. But before she could speak she heard her name and turned to see Rafa hurrying toward her.

"You came!" he said with a happy smile. "It was getting late and I thought you'd changed your mind."

"We had some last-minute work at the office," April explained. "I wouldn't miss your debut for anything."

"Especially since you're so fond of bullfighting," Alejandro said dryly.

April shot him a look, then hooked her arm through Rafa's. "Excited?"

"Yes!"

"Terrified?"

He looked surprised. "How did you know?"

With a laugh, feeling better than she had in days, April hugged him close to her. "Stage fright," she said. "We all have it, whether it's bullfighting or a first date or a new job. If you weren't ready for this, Alejandro wouldn't let you fight. You're going to do fine."

"If you look as handsome tomorrow as you look

tonight, you're going to do better than fine," Pepita said. "I'm not sure which of your uncles you look like. They're both handsome, but you're better-looking than either of them."

"That's enough," Alejandro put in. "He's already impossibly spoiled." He put his hand on Rafa's shoulder and said, "Let's introduce the ladies to the others."

Aunts and uncles, a cousin or two, Rafa's brother Manuel and his wife. And finally Doña Inez, Alejandro's grandmother.

When he led April to the white-haired woman, he said, *"Abuela,* I would like you to meet the Señorita April Juneau from the United States. April, this is my grandmother."

Señora Inez Gabriela Garcia Cervantes was a handsome dark-skinned woman in her late seventies. In spite of the lines of age in her face she was still a regally handsome woman. Though her face had aged, her eyes had not. They were the same wonderful Gypsy green as Alejandro's.

"Señora," said April, taking the old lady's hand, "Alejandro has told me about you. I'm very happy to meet you."

"Please sit beside me. I would like to know you better." She waved Alejandro away with an imperious hand and said, "Go entertain your other guests. I will take care of Señorita Juneau." When he had gone she turned to April and said, "Now then, we will chat. Do you like Spain?"

"Yes, very much."

"How long have you been here?"

"Over a year, *señora.*"

"And will you stay?"

"No, I'm going back to the United States in a few months."

"But why? I thought you said you like it here."

"I do, but—"

"Are you in love with Alejandro?"

"Doña Inez, really, I—"

"Don't pussyfoot, young lady. I've asked you a direct question. I want to know if you're in love with my grandson."

April hesitated a moment more, then said, "Yes, *señora*, I am in love with Alejandro."

"That's what I thought. It's obvious that Alec is in love with you. It's also obvious that the two of you have a problem. He's been behaving exactly the way his grandfather used to behave when he couldn't get his way: taciturn and bad-tempered." She reached out and took April's hand in hers. "It's the bulls, isn't it? That's what is keeping you apart."

It was the understanding in her voice that brought the mist of tears to April's eyes. She bit her lip and looked away from Doña Inez, trying to regain her composure, then felt the pressure of the old lady's hands squeezing hers.

"You must not let him go." The whispered words were fierce. "Marry him and then fight with him if you must. But don't let him go."

"People . . . people have to solve their problems before they marry, Doña Inez."

"Nonsense!" She leaned closer and, in a conspiratorial whisper, said, "You have a Catholic wedding and then you are together forever. That is all that counts. You sleep beside him every night, you have his children. Then you nag him. Then you fight and threaten."

In spite of herself April smiled. "I don't think that's quite fair, *señora*. And I'm not sure it would work with Alejandro. Our problem is not a simple one."

"Love is never simple, my dear. I have a feeling in

my heart that you and Alejandro belong together.
Marry him and then fight for him."

"That wouldn't be honest."

"Dios! I knew you'd say that. Well, we shall see, yes?
But please, don't give up on that stubborn grandson of
mine." The green eyes twinkled. "If I have to, I'll put a
Gypsy spell on him."

"I wouldn't put it past you," April said with a laugh.

Several times during the evening she looked up to see
Alejandro's eyes on her, his dark brows pulled together
in a frown. When they finished dinner and Doña Inez,
Rafa and several of the aunts and uncles had said their
good nights, he said to April, "What did you and my
grandmother talk about?"

"Gypsy spells," April said with a slight smile.

He frowned and looked away.

"She's quite a woman, Alec. I'm glad I had the
opportunity to meet her."

"I'm glad you were able to come." He hesitated.
"May I drive you back to your hotel?"

"I thought I'd wait for Esteban and Pepita."

"They've decided to look for some music and have a
few drinks. Would you care to join them?"

"Not really."

"Then come along." Alejandro took her arm and,
after she had said good night to the others, walked her
out to the Mercedes.

They were silent in the car. Without asking, he drove
away from the city, and when April said, "Where are
we going?" he said, "I thought you might like to see the
Alcázar by moonlight."

When April nodded he drove out to the junction of
the two rivers that ran near Segovia, turned his car
around so that it faced the city and pulled to the side of
the road.

The Alcázar stood on the crest of a hill, shining in the moonlight, a fairy-tale castle from another century. This was the castle where Isabella lived when she first met Ferdinand, and it was from here that she was called upon to become queen.

This was Spain, April thought as she gazed up at the old stone structure. Land of enchantment and romance, of stately beauty and past glories. A country so rich in history that it staggered the mind.

On a night like this she belonged to Spain. She could feel the rhythm and the mystery of the ages and see it in the face of the man who sat next to her. For Alejandro was Spain, the blood of all her people: the Iberians and Celts, Romans and Visigoths and Muslims, ran in his veins. Alejandro was the pride and the beauty, the arrogance and the brutality and the strength, that was Spain. The Spain she loved, just as she loved Alejandro Cervantes.

They sat for a long time without speaking. Finally he started the car and drove her back to her hotel.

When he unlocked her door and handed her the key, he said, "You look very beautiful tonight, April."

"Thank you." She waited, aware of the frantic beat of pulse in her throat, wondering what she would do if Alejandro pulled her into his arms.

But he didn't. April saw the strain in his face, the nervous jump of muscle in his jaw. In a low voice he said, "Have you changed your mind about anything?"

"No." The word was a whisper. "I'm sorry."

"So am I."

And before she could speak again, he turned on his heel and disappeared down the hotel corridor.

The *corrida* was a *mano a mano* between Alejandro and Domingo Reyes. They would each fight three bulls.

Then Rafael would fight a *novillo*, a young bull. The two senior matadors wore their suits of lights, but Rafa wore a light gray *traje corto*. He was in the *callejón* with them during the fight, looking very serious and intense, and older than his almost fifteen years.

There were some twenty-odd relatives grouped together in the front rows. Doña Inez had insisted that April sit with her. "I feel about the bulls just as you do," she said. "We will suffer together."

When Alejandro stepped into the ring to receive his first bull, April could feel Doña Inez tense. And when he dropped to his knees and called the bull to him, when the great white horns passed within inches of his face, she could hear the hiss of breath in the grandmother's throat. April reached for Doña Inez's hand.

"This is the first time in ten years that I have seen Alec fight. I vowed the last time that I would never do this again. But I had to be here today because of Rafael." Her voice was sad. "Now I will have two of them to pray for."

Alejandro wore the same silver-encrusted black satin suit of lights that he had worn the first time April had ever seen him. And as she had that first day, she thought how magnificent he was, how slim and tall and graceful. Then she'd been excited by the *corrida*. She'd shouted *olé*'s and *bravo*'s with the rest of the crowd, cheering him on, applauding his bravery.

But she hadn't loved him then.

He cut the ears on his first bull. His second animal was not good. He got as much out of it as he could, then dispatched it quickly and cleanly. His third bull was the kind of an animal a matador prays for. Even April, with all her fear, understood how really brilliant Alejandro was.

He played the bull, calling him closer and closer to

his body, doing beautiful things as he dominated this great proud beast. At the close of the *faena* he asked for an *indulto*, a pardon for the bull. When the authority agreed, the oxen came to lead the bull out to where his wounds would be healed. As he was led from the ring, the people stood and called, "*Toro, Toro, Toro.*"

Then Alejandro was awarded the symbolic ears and tail and took a tour of the ring as the crowd shouted his name and threw their hats, *botas* of wine and flowers. He looked up and saw his grandmother and April together when he passed under their *barrera*. His eyes went from one face to the other with a look that was both searching and intense.

Then his grandmother threw the red roses she had brought and called "*Bravo, Alec! Bravo!*" before he moved to the center of the ring to take his final bow, this time with the *ganadero*, the rancher from whose ranch the bulls had come today.

When he came back to the *barrera* Alejandro put his hand on Rafa's shoulder and said something to the boy. Rafa looked up at him, his face tense with eagerness, as he nodded.

The crowd waited. The *toril* was thrown open and suddenly, with the force of a small train, the young bull exploded into the ring.

One of Alejandro's *banderilleros* studied the animal for a moment, then he dashed into the arena to test the charge of the bull.

When he jumped behind the *barrera* he nodded to Rafa and the boy, looking tight-lipped and eager, ran into the ring, shouting, "*Ahaaa, toro! Ahaaa!*"

The young bull charged. Rafa stood his ground, swirling his cape in a perfect *verónica*. Another and another, each better than the last, the yellow and magenta cape moving in perfect rhythm. Rafa's feet, looking as though they were anchored in the sand, did not move. The delicate boyish body swayed with the cape, doing all the things Alejandro had taught him, his movements graceful and aesthetic. He twisted from the waist to follow the cape with chest and turn of face. Smooth, unhurried, nerveless.

The crowd jumped to their feet, cheering as the boy did pass after pass. And April, because she had said she would, shouted *"Olé!"* and applauded with the rest of them.

Rafa looked so young, she thought, with his boyish face and thin neck, which gave him a look of touching vulnerability. She thought of how he had looked that day at Alejandro's ranch when he'd been hurt. He hadn't liked her then, and she wondered now if it had been because he had thought she might steal a part of Alejandro's love.

"I think he will be very good," Doña Inez said. "He has the gift, eh? That indescribable something, the art and the grace."

Alejandro, standing at the *barrera*, every muscle tensed and ready to spring into the ring if Rafa needed him, knew it too—knew that if Rafa continued to be serious about the profession, if he worked hard, if he trained and did all the things he should do, he would one day be a great matador.

It was during the *faena*, the last part of the fight, that the fear came to Alejandro. One moment he was all right and the next moment his stomach was knotted with a fear so terrible that it left him shaking and weak.

The boy had tried a *pase de pecho*. When the animal's horns came close to Rafa's thin chest, Alejandro felt the sweat break out on his face and trickle down his arms.

Then, a moment later, Rafa tried a *trincherazo*, the red cape and the sword held low in his right hand as he called the bull slowly from right to left.

But something went wrong. The snout of the bull caught Rafa and he fell.

Before the bull could reach him, Alejandro was in the ring, calling the bull, luring him away with his own body.

"I'm all right!" Rafa called, jumping to his feet, motioning Alejandro away.

Hands curled so tightly around his cape that the knuckles were white, Alejandro nodded and went, walking slowly backward, never taking his eyes off Rafa, to the side of the *burladero*.

Christ! He wanted to throw Rafa over his shoulder and carry him out of the ring. He wanted to beat him until he promised he would never fight another bull. He wanted to get down on his knees and beg the boy to give it up. Silently he cursed himself for having taught Rafa what he knew and swore that never again would he help a boy to enter the profession.

But it was too late for Rafa. It was in his blood now and he would never give it up, because he was good. Some day, with luck, he might even be great.

When it was over, when Rafa made his victorious tour of the ring, his young face was flushed with pride as he smiled up at the crowd. With a poise that went far beyond his years, he accepted the adulation, letting his *cuadrilla* carry the flowers that were thrown down to him. But when he came to where his family and April were and she tossed a bouquet of red roses down to him, he picked them up off the sand and carried them the rest of the way around the ring.

* * *

For the celebration in Alejandro's hotel suite after the *corrida* April changed to a black velvet pantsuit, a white satin shirt and black high-heeled pumps. She wore her red hair loose around her shoulders, held back from her face with a black velvet band.

When she pushed the door open she was surprised by the number of people crowded into the room, by the flow of talk and the loudness of the music. Then it was as though a path had opened and she saw Alejandro. He was sitting on a sofa surrounded by women.

It was almost, April thought, as though a piece of film had been rolled backward. Nothing had changed. It was as though she had never existed.

Alejandro raised his head and saw her. For a moment his face froze and his body tensed as he moved to get up, but then his eyes narrowed and he looked away from her. He rested back against the sofa as he turned to say something to one of the women sitting next to him.

Chapter 15

"HOW COULD YOU? YOU PROMISED ME!"

"Just listen for a minute."

"I've listened to you for the last time!"

Heads were raised. People stared, looked embarrassed, then pretended to go back to the papers on their desks.

April, who had just come out of her office, hesitated. Then, as the angry voices continued, she hurried to Esteban's office and rapped. When he barked an angry "Who is it?" she opened the door and went in.

"What in the world is the matter with you two?" she said in a low voice. "The whole office can hear you."

"I don't give a damn about the office," Pepita shouted.

"Lower your voice," Esteban said.

"Don't tell me what to do."

"Nobody can tell you anything. I'd like to shake some sense into you!"

"Shake some sense into *me!* You're the one who—"

"Stop it!" April's voice cracked like a whip in the room. "Both of you stop it this instant. Pepita, sit down and shut up." When the other girl tried to speak, April held up a warning hand and said, "One more word and you're out of a job. I mean it."

The other girl glared at her. "You call yourself my friend," she mumbled under her breath.

"I'm also your boss and I'm telling you to stop this immediately."

When Pepita sat down, her face tense with anger, April turned to Esteban and said, "What's this all about?"

"I've just seen Alvarez. I've resigned."

"I see." April leaned against the edge of his desk.

"And I've just broken the engagement," Pepita snapped. "He lied to me. He promised to give the job here a fair try."

"I did give it a fair try," Esteban said, "but I'm not cut out for office work." He turned to April. "If she'd just give the vineyard a chance, she'd learn to like it."

"I'll never learn to like it," Pepita said, "because I'm not going to spend even one day sitting on that lousy piece of land of yours."

"It isn't a lousy piece of land." Esteban's face was white with anger. "You refuse to even give it a chance."

"That's right!" Pepita jumped up from her chair and faced him. "Make up your mind right now, Esteban," she said in a cold flat voice. "Either you go in there and tell Alvarez you've changed your mind or we're through."

"You don't mean that."

"Try me!"

They stared at each other, their faces tense and angry. Then Esteban shook his head, and before either of the women could say a word, he turned and walked out of the office.

"Go after him," April said.

Pepita's nostrils flared with anger.

"Don't let him go like this," April pleaded.

"He can go," Pepita said. "He can go straight to hell."

They stared at each other across Esteban's desk. Then, with a sigh, knowing there was nothing left to say, April went out and shut the office door.

She wanted to shake Pepita. She wanted to beg the girl not to let Esteban go. But Pepita would not have listened, just as she, April, hadn't listened when Alejandro's grandmother said, "Marry him and *then* fight with him. But don't let him go."

Now it was too late. April had known the weekend before, when Alejandro looked up at her from the sofa, that she had lost him, that he had put her out of his life and that he had allowed other women—women who would not be as difficult as she had been, who would not ask too much of him—back into his life.

All that was left was the memory of a summer when they had loved each other.

April and Pepita barely spoke to each other during the next few days. Pepita talked to Señor Alvarez about transferring to the New York office. Then Alvarez called April in to ask if she still intended to keep Pepita as her secretary when she went back to the United States.

"No," April said. "I think Pepita has grown beyond that. Why don't you give her a chance in sales? If she can improve her English in the next few months, I think she'd fit in nicely with the New York sales staff."

When Alvarez agreed, April suggested that he transfer Pepita to sales immediately.

"I'll only be here a few more months," she said. "Any of the women from the typing pool can act as my secretary."

He looked at her thoughtfully. "You know, April, I wish you'd change your mind about returning to New York. You're doing a fine job for us here. I spoke to Señor Montez about you yesterday and he agrees that we'd be more than happy if you changed your mind and decided to stay here with us."

He smiled at her across his big desk. "That foreign-sales job is open now that Esteban has resigned. We're prepared to offer it and the vice-presidency to you if you decide to stay."

"I don't know what to say, Señor Alvarez. I've made up my mind to return to the States. I—I appreciate your offer, but . . ."

"I don't want an answer now. Think about it for a week or two. We're in no hurry. We'll talk about this again next week."

At any other time April thought that night when she was alone in her apartment, she would have jumped at the vice-presidency. It was not often, especially in Spain, that a woman was offered such a prestigious job. But the thought of staying in Spain and not being able to see Alejandro was too painful. She'd be better off in her own country.

She read for a long time that night, and it was late before she finally fell asleep. It seemed that she had no more than turned the light off when the phone rang.

Fumbling for the light, she reached for the phone and, in a voice fogged by sleep, said, "Yes? Hello?"

"April!"

"Pepita? Is that you?"

"April, please . . ."

"What's the matter? What is it?"

Pepita was crying so hard it was difficult to understand what she said.

"What is it?" April said again.

"Esteban."

"What? What do you mean?"

"Esteban—" The other girl sobbed into the phone.

"Has something happened to him?"

"An accident. Oh, my God, April. He's been in an accident."

"Where? Is he all right?" April sat up in bed, pushing her hair out of her face as she fought to remain calm.

"Near Seville. I've got to get to him."

"Yes. All right. Look, I'll call the airport and then I'll call you back."

"Will you come to Seville with me?"

"Yes, of course." She hesitated. "How serious is it?"

"The man . . . the man who called me from the hospital said—" Her voice choked with sobs. "—he said Esteban was critical. He said they didn't know. Oh, April. April!"

"Hang on. Don't even think that he's not going to be all right. Just pack your suitcase and get dressed. I'll call you back as soon as I make our reservations."

April phoned the airport and made reservations for an early-morning flight to Seville. Then she called Pepita to tell her to be at the airport at seven the next morning.

And finally, almost without conscious thought, she phoned La Esperanza.

The phone rang for a long time, and suddenly, holding the receiver against her ear, April's hands began to shake almost uncontrollably. When she heard Alejandro's voice, it was all she could do to say, "This is April."

"April? Are you all right?"

"Yes. It's . . . it's Esteban, Alejandro. There's been an accident."

"Is it serious?"

"I think so."

"Where is he?"

"Seville. Pepita and I are flying there in the morning. But I thought . . ." She swallowed, trying to regain her composure. "I thought you could get there sooner."

"I'll leave right away."

"Alejandro." Her mouth was so dry she could barely speak. "Alejandro, they had a fight. If anything happens to him . . ."

"Don't even think that way!" She could hear the harshness of his voice. "I'll see you in the morning, April."

"Yes. Yes, all right." Slowly she put the phone down.

There was rain the next morning and the plane was late leaving. Pepita, her face pinched and white, sat in the waiting room, twisting her fingers nervously together in her lap.

"What time is it?" she asked again and again. "When are we going to leave? Ask them, April. Ask them what the hell has happened to the plane?"

"I did just a minute ago, Pepita. It won't be long now. There's fog, they said, but it's lifting. We should be able to take off anytime."

"April, ask them. Please."

So once again April went to the flight information desk. When she came back she said, "We'll be boarding in ten minutes."

"Thank God. If I have to sit here any longer I'll go crazy."

The flight, once they were above the rain clouds, was fairly smooth. Pepita refused breakfast when it was served, but she drank two cups of coffee. After she had she closed her eyes and leaned back against her seat.

"It's my fault," she said finally.

"No, it's not. It was an accident."

"Esteban wouldn't have left if it hadn't been for me. He'd still be at the office. He'd be safe."

"Pepita." April covered the other girl's hands with hers.

"He always drove too fast in that damned sports car of his. I've hated that car from the day he bought it. *Madre de Dios,* April. If anything happens to him . . ."

Tears streamed down her face, and April felt her own throat constrict with the need to cry.

Because there was only one morning flight between Madrid and Seville, April had expected to see Alejandro at the airport. When she didn't she felt a nudge of uneasiness. She and Pepita had brought only carry-on luggage, so as soon as they left the plane, they signaled for a taxi and went right to the hospital. They asked for Esteban's room and were told they could go up.

Alejandro saw them as soon as they stepped off the elevator. He kissed Pepita and said, "There's a waiting room just down here. Why don't we leave your bags there? Was the flight all right? Have you had breakfast?"

And while he had not spoken directly to April, his hand had reached for hers the moment he saw her and did not let go.

"How is he?" Pepita's voice was impatient. "Can I see him?"

"Not right now, dear. Why don't you sit down."

"Why can't I see him?" Her voice rose.

"Because the doctor is with him now." Alejandro's hand tightened on April's. "He's badly hurt, Pepita."

"Ay, Madre!" She looked at him with desperate eyes. "How badly, Alejandro?"

He shook his head. "We'll know more after the doctor sees him."

"Does anyone know what happened?" April asked.

"It was near Carmona, on the outskirts of Seville. Esteban was driving too fast. Apparently he'd been drinking. There was a hay wagon ahead of him, and when he tried to pass it, he went out of control. He was thrown out of the car."

Pepita closed her eyes and swayed. Alejandro reached for her and led her to a sofa. "Easy," he said. "Easy now."

"It's my fault," she whispered. "I sent him away, Alejandro. I told him I wouldn't marry him."

The door to Esteban's room opened and a gray-haired man with a white coat over his stooped shoulders came out.

"That's the doctor," Alejandro said. "Wait here while I talk to him."

Quickly, April moved to take his place beside Pepita on the sofa. She put her arm around the other girl's shoulders as she watched Alejandro and the doctor. The doctor's face was serious. He pulled on his heavy mustache, nodding at Alejandro's questions, then shaking his head, lifting his shoulders in a shrug. Alejandro said something and the doctor glanced at Pepita and nodded.

When the doctor turned away, Alejandro hurried back to the two women and said, "You can see Esteban now, Pepita. But he probably won't know you're there. He's in and out most of the time."

"What did the doctor say? Is he going to be all right?" Her dark eyes were anxious.

"He doesn't know. But then, he doesn't know Esteban like we do. Would you like us to go in with you?"

"Yes, please."

Alejandro opened the door and the three of them moved silently into the room.

Esteban's head was swathed in bandages. His face, except for the black and blue patches under his eyes, was as white as the sheet that covered him. One arm was in a cast and there were bandages across his chest. His eyes were closed and his breathing was shallow.

Pepita reached for April's hand and, squeezing hard, approached the bed. "Esteban," she whispered. "Esteban? Can you hear me, *querido?* It's Pepita, darling."

He didn't move or open his eyes.

"Oh, Esteban," she said, and began to weep.

Behind her Alejandro pulled a chair close to the bed. "Why don't you sit with him for a while?" he said as he eased her into the chair.

She nodded, unable to speak. Looking up at Alejandro with tear-filled eyes, she managed to say, "I think I'd like to be alone with him, please."

"Of course. We'll be right outside if you want anything."

He held the door for April and when they were outside he said, "Are you all right? You look pretty shaky."

"I *am* pretty shaky."

"Would you like some coffee?"

"Maybe later." She looked at him, her eyes serious. "What did the doctor say, Alejandro?"

He took a deep breath. "He said that he didn't know for sure whether or not Esteban was going to make it."

"Oh, God." April clenched her hands, trying desperately to steady herself.

"But he's got a chance, April. I've asked the doctor to call in a neurosurgeon. He's flying in from Madrid this afternoon. I want another opinion."

"Yes." She nodded. "That's good."

"My grandmother wanted to come with me last night, but I wouldn't let her."

"She's at La Esperanza?"

"Yes. She came back with Rafa and me after the *corrida*." He smiled his wry smile. "I don't know what you did to her, but all she's done since she's been at the ranch is give me hell. You know, all these years the story has been that my grandfather kidnapped her. Now I'm not so sure. It might have been the other way around."

"I wouldn't be surprised. She offered to put a Gypsy spell on you."

"I'll be damned! That wicked old woman!"

"Wicked, maybe, but terribly sweet. I wish she were my grandmother."

"We could arrange that, you know."

April looked away from him. "We've made our decisions, Alejandro. Let's stick by them."

"She told me I ought to drag you to a priest, force you to marry me, *then* fight with you."

"She told me the same thing. That's ridiculous, of course."

"That's what I told her." His gaze held hers. "But she's a stubborn old woman, April. She thinks love is reason enough for marriage."

"Alejandro . . . please."

He took a deep breath and looked away from her.

They were silent for a long time and finally April said, "Would you check on Esteban, please?"

He nodded, and in a few minutes he came back and said, "Pepita wants to stay with him. She says it's all

right if you go in now. I'd like to phone grandmother
and Rafa and let them know how Esteban is. They can
phone the other relatives. Will you be all right? Can I
get you some coffee?"

When she shook her head he left her and she went
into Esteban's room.

Day passed slowly into evening. Nurses moved silently in and out of the room. Alejandro brought
sandwiches, but no one ate them.

When the neurosurgeon arrived from Madrid, he
asked them to leave the room while he examined
Esteban. April and Pepita sat side by side on the sofa;
Alejandro paced up and down in front of them.

When the surgeon came out he said, "I've seen the X
rays and I've examined him. There are bone splinters
near the brain. I'd like to operate. I'll need somebody's
permission."

"Operate?" Pepita's face was the color of ashes.

"There is really no choice, *señorita*. Are you a
member of the family?"

"No. I'm . . . I'm his fiancée."

"I'll have to get written consent from somebody."

"I'm his cousin," Alejandro said. He looked at
Pepita. "If you agree, then I'll sign the papers."

She seemed not to be able to draw a breath. Then
finally she nodded and, in a trembling voice, said,
"Thank you, Alejandro. Yes, sign them. We've got to
try."

It was the longest night that April ever spent. When
Esteban was wheeled away, Pepita broke down and
became hysterical. The floor nurse, on the instructions
of the doctor, gave her a sedative and put her to bed.
April and Alejandro sat in the waiting room, jumping
up every time they heard a step in the corridor. Finally,
exhausted, April curled up in one corner of the sofa

and went to sleep, only to be awakened a short time later when Alejandro said, "The doctor is coming."

April reached for his hand and together they went to meet the surgeon.

The man looked tired, but there was a suggestion of a smile on his face. "I think he's going to make it," he said.

"Thank God." April was limp with relief and felt Alejandro's arm encircle her waist.

"He's still unconscious. I can't tell you when he'll wake up. It may be hours, it may be several days. We'll know a lot more then than we do now."

"Thank you, doctor. Thank you for everything," Alejandro said.

"I have some things to do in Seville, Señor Cervantes, so I will be around for a few days. I'll look in on Señor Davalos later today."

"I'm going to take you to a hotel," Alejandro said when the doctor had gone. "You're exhausted."

"All right, but let me see Pepita first."

While Alejandro waited, she went into the room where Pepita was and, after a moment's hesitation, touched the other woman's shoulder.

Pepita's eyes flew open. "What is it?" She grasped April's arm. "Is he all right? Is he . . . ?"

"He came through the operation and the doctor thinks he's going to be all right."

"Thank God." Her dark eyes flooded with tears. "Can I see him?"

"Not now. He's in the recovery room. It may be hours before he wakes up. If you promise you'll rest here, I won't insist that you go to a hotel."

"I promise."

"You'll try to go back to sleep now?"

"Yes, April."

"All right, then. I'll take our luggage and check us into a hotel." She leaned over the bed and kissed Pepita's cheek. "He's going to be all right, Pep," she whispered. "I know he is."

The sun was coming up when she and Alejandro drove through the streets of Seville to the Alfonso XIII Hotel, where Alejandro had reserved three rooms. Although April was so tired she could barely speak, he insisted she eat and managed to get soft-boiled eggs and toast from the kitchen. When they had eaten he took her to her room.

"I want to get back to the hospital as soon as I can," she said. "I'll leave a call for noon."

"You don't need to. I'll call you."

"All right. You get some rest too."

"I will."

April wanted to touch him, wanted to lean her head against his shoulder and have him put his arms around her and tell her that everything was all right.

If he made one step toward her. If he touched her.

But he didn't, and with a brief good night April went into her room and closed the door.

Chapter 16

THREE DAYS PASSED AND STILL ESTEBAN DID NOT REGAIN consciousness.

Alejandro returned to La Esperanza and brought his grandmother and Rafa to Seville. Doña Inez, after one harsh flood of tears, was calm and controlled. She insisted Pepita eat, saying that the girl would be of no help to Esteban when he awoke if she allowed herself to get ill. Pepita resented the old lady's interference but did as she was told, half afraid that Doña Inez would force-feed her if she refused.

When she was not with Esteban, Doña Inez spent much of her time with April. She did not speak of April's relationship with Alejandro, but instead told her stories of the family, of Alejandro's mother and father and of his grandfather.

"Alejandro looks like me," she said, "but he has his grandfather's temperament."

"How did you meet your husband?" April asked.

"I was riding one of our horses. I wasn't supposed to, of course, because the horse was almost as wild as I was. But it was spring and the air was alive with magic.

I rode like the wind, making the horse go faster and faster. Suddenly a rider came up over the crest of a hill in front of me. I almost collided with him."

She laughed softly, remembering. "I pulled up in time, but I was so furious that I shouted at him and I'm afraid I called him all kinds of a fool. Then I calmed down and looked at him—really looked at him—and I wanted to kill myself! *Madre de Dios!* I had never seen a man to equal him. He sat there, looking like a king on his black stallion, wearing fancy leather boots, dressed in the most elegant riding outfit I had ever seen, laughing at me. Me in my Gypsy dress and bare feet, my hair all tangled by the wind.

"Did you say anything? Did he?"

"No! I was so embarrassed, so impressed by how handsome and elegant he was, that all I could do was stare at him. Then I turned my horse and rode in the other direction as though the Devil himself were after me.

"But Armando—that was his name, Armando—he followed me to where we were camped. I hid in my mother's wagon and he began to talk to some of the men. He came back the next day and again he talked to the men, but he kept staring at me. When my mother told me to go down to the river for water, he followed me." She leaned close to April. "Armando kissed me, there by the river. It was the first time a man's lips had ever touched mine.

"He came back to the camp every day for a week, and every night I met him down by the river. Then it was time for us to move on and I thought I would die, because I didn't want to leave him. But he had no intention of leaving me, April. He went to my brothers and asked for my hand, just as though I'd been a lady of quality. And when my brothers said no, that Gypsies only married Gypsies, Armando threw me on his horse and kidnapped me."

So the story Alejandro had told of the kidnapping was true: His grandfather really had taken his grandmother by force.

"But you went willingly, didn't you?" April asked. "I mean, if you loved him . . . ?"

"Willingly?" The old lady laughed. "No, of course not. I fought like a tiger. I scratched and kicked and made a terrible fuss. But I'd have killed him if he had let me go."

Impulsively, April hugged Doña Inez. "You're wonderful," she said with a little laugh. "I think I love you."

"And I love you, child. I only wish . . ."

"I know."

"No Gypsy spells?"

"I don't think they'd help."

When Alejandro took his grandmother and Rafa back to the ranch, April spent all of her time with Pepita. The girl, who had kept an almost constant vigil at Esteban's bedside, had changed in the week since the accident. All of the brightness of her beauty and the color of her personality seemed to have faded from spending hour after endless hour beside Esteban's bed. And as the hours and the days went by, her face grew more pinched, her eyes more hopeless.

The neurosurgeon, after a consultation with Alejandro, returned to Madrid.

"There's nothing more I can do," he'd said. "It's in God's hands now."

Late one afternoon, as the October sun slanted through the blinds, Pepita fell asleep, Esteban's hand still clasped in hers, her head resting on the bed.

As April watched them she felt quick tears spring to

her eyes. If Esteban dies, she thought, Pepita will never forgive herself. She'll carry a terrible guilt for the rest of her life.

Leaning her head back against the chair, eyes closed, April whispered, "Please let him live. Let them have a chance to share a life together."

For a few moments it seemed that she drifted into a restful sleep. Then she opened her eyes and looked at Esteban. His eyelids fluttered. The tip of his tongue moistened the corner of his mouth. The hand that Pepita held twitched.

In a voice she could scarcely recognize as her own, April whispered, "Pepita! Pepita!"

The dark head raised from the bed and she glanced at April. When she saw the expression on April's face, she turned back to the bed and saw the faint flutter of lids.

"Esteban?" The whispered joyful cry tumbled from her lips. "Esteban? Darling, can you hear me?"

"Pepita?" The word was so faint that April could barely hear it as she moved to stand closer to the bed.

"Yes, Esteban. Open your eyes, darling."

He did. He opened them and looked up at Pepita and said, "There was an accident."

"Yes, dear."

"My head hurts."

"I know." She leaned to kiss him. "But it will be better soon."

"You won't leave?"

"No, darling. I won't leave. Not now. Not ever."

As April turned away, blinded by tears, she stumbled out the door and into Alejandro's arms.

"He's awake," she said, weeping. "He's going to be all right." She felt the comfort of his body as he pulled her close and whispered, "Thank God. Thank God."

Pepita wouldn't leave the hospital. "I want to be here

when he wakes up again," she said. "I'm all right now, truly I am. The nurse is going to bring me a blanket. I'll put the chair back and sleep. You go back to the hotel, April. I know how tired you are."

She was tired—so tired that she didn't argue when Alejandro walked her to her room and went in with her.

"You'll feel better after you've had some hot food," he said.

"I think I'll just go to bed."

"Nonsense." His voice was firm. Before she could object, he picked up the phone and ordered two bowls of soup and a pot of tea. Then he went into the bathroom, and when he had run a tub, he came back to find her asleep at the foot of the bed.

"Come on," he ordered, "off with your clothes and into the tub."

April glared at him through sleepy eyes. Then, mumbling under her breath, she made her way into the bathroom and shucked off her clothes.

She had just settled into the hot water when Alejandro tapped at the door and, without waiting for a reply, entered with a tray, which he set on a stool near the tub.

"Eat all of it," he said with authority.

Half angry and half amused, April ate the soup, then finished bathing. By the time she had slipped into her gown, she felt almost human.

"Feel better?" Alejandro asked when she came back into the bedroom.

April glanced at him, noting that he'd taken off his jacket and tie and opened his shirt. "Yes," she said. "The soup was good. Thank you, Alec. I'll—I'll see you in the morning."

His green eyes searched her face. "I have to go back to the ranch tomorrow, April. I'll stop in and see Esteban before I go, but if he's all right, I'll spend the day at the ranch. Rufino came in from Geneva yesterday and I want to get him settled in.

"How is he?"

"He's fine. Rafa told me Rufino walks almost as fast as he does. And he's full of plans. He says we're going to make La Esperanza the greatest brave-bull ranch in the world."

"I hope he's right, Alejandro."

"So do I. Sometimes I wish I could spend more time there than I do." He hesitated. "I wish you could take a few more days off and spend them at La Esperanza."

"I'm afraid I can't. I have to get back to Madrid. I'm—I'm going back to the States sooner than I thought and I have a lot of things to take care of."

"I'll be leaving soon, too, for South America. I suppose this . . . this is good-bye."

April's throat ached with the need to cry, but she managed to say, "Yes, I suppose so."

"A kiss for remembrance?"

"I don't think so, Alec."

A muscle jumped in his cheek. "I do."

And before April could back away, he pulled her to him, locking her in his arms so tightly that she couldn't breathe. Then his mouth, searching and hungry, found hers.

She knew that she was lost and told herself that this was the last time, the last time Alejandro would ever kiss her. She almost wept when he let her go.

He looked down at her, his eyes narrowing as he studied her face. Then, with a low growl of desire, he swept her up into his arms and carried her to the bed.

When he put her down he tore the rest of his clothes off.

"No," April whispered. "We said—"

"I don't give a damn what we said." He lay down beside her and gathered her in his arms. "That's not important. This is. Being with you is all that matters."

"No!" She tried to struggle out of his arms. "You have your other women, I saw you. I—"

"That's nonsense and you know it."

"No, I—"

But he stopped the words with his mouth, which demanded response as his lips parted and his tongue touched hers, seeking the warm recesses of her mouth. His hands pressed her close to him, trying to slip inside the gown to touch her breasts. Then, as though frantic with impatience, he put his hands at the top of her gown and ripped it from her body, stopping her protests with his mouth.

His hands roamed freely as the satin cloth fell away. He cupped her breasts and leaned to kiss them, to take each tender tip between his teeth while his tongue teased it to readiness.

Slowly, insidiously, April felt the tide of passion glide over her body, warming her, carrying her to a crest of desire where nothing mattered except this moment in Alejandro's arms. Tomorrow he would leave her, but she would have tonight to remember.

Her arms crept around his neck to caress the soft hairs at the back of his head, to knead the muscles of his shoulders as her fingers moved slowly down his back to touch his round, firm buttocks. She wanted him. Oh, Lord, how she wanted him.

But as she lifted her body to his, he said, "Not yet, April. Not yet, my love." Then he covered one of her breasts with his mouth, warming it, circling the taut nipple with his tongue, nibbling when it peaked to hardness.

It went on and on, his mouth warm against her flesh while his hands caressed her until her body was on fire with longing, until each breath was a whimper of desire and she pressed her body to his, whispering, "Please, Alejandro. Please, now, darling."

But he only shook his head, and when she tried to pull away, his teeth clamped on the nipple, stopping her, making her gasp for a moment before he soothed it with his tongue, and went on to drive her to further madness.

Suddenly, his hands gripping her arms, he rolled onto his back, pulling her on top of him. Then his hands sought her hair and he lifted her face to his.

"Do you know how much I've wanted you?" he demanded hoarsely. "Do you know how many nights I've lain awake, aching with the need of you? Do you know how I'm aching now, making myself wait because I know this is all we're ever going to have?"

His fingers tightened in her hair. "There've been no other women, April. I didn't want a substitute; I only wanted you." He pulled her face down to his in a kiss that left her breathless. Then with a cry he rolled her onto her back and entered her.

It had never been this intense, this overpowering. He held her with his arms and his body and his legs, which were like iron as his body moved against hers.

No, a part of April's mind protested. This is too much. "No," she cried, even as her body moved against Alejandro's, frantic with need now as her body lifted to his. Her hands pressed against the small of his back to urge him closer. Her nails dug into his flesh. She was frantic with feeling, unaware of anything except his body, which possessed her, driving her wild with desire as she climbed the high peaks of ecstasy.

She wanted to cry out her love for him, wanted to tell him that she would love him until the day she died. But she wouldn't, she couldn't, not even when her hungry mouth rained kisses on his face and his strong throat, then moved to his shoulder, tasting his skin, biting in frantic need as he moved faster against her.

Then finally, finally, when April could bear no more, she cried his name and, lifting her body to his, burst through her desire into myriad rainbow-colored lights. She cried out again as she felt him shudder against her and heard his frenzied whisper of her name against her lips.

Trembling, April burrowed her head against his shoulder and clung to him as though she would never let him go.

He smoothed the damp hair away from her face and, after a moment, said, "I think my grandmother is right, love. I think we should marry and then do our fighting."

She stiffened in his arms.

"You know I love you, April."

"And I love you, Alejandro. But—"

"But not enough to accept me the way I am." His voice had gone flat.

"I'm sorry," she whispered against his chest.

When she tried to move out of his arms, he held her. And after a while, still curled against the warmth of him, she fell asleep.

He was gone when April awoke the next morning. On the stand next to the bed there was a small box wrapped in white tissue paper and tied with a red ribbon. Inside, on a bed of cotton, lay a small gold fan.

April looked at it and at the charm bracelet she'd taken off the night before. The bracelet was, as Alejandro had promised, heavy with charms: a tiny wine goblet from Jerez, a castle from Segovia, a sailboat from Valencia, a rose from Granada.

With trembling fingers she picked up the fan. She knew that this was the last charm Alejandro would ever give her.

Chapter 17

It seemed odd to April that Madrid, a city she had grown to love, now looked so bleak and lifeless. She took no pleasure in the broad avenues, the tree-lined boulevards or the lovely old buildings. Once she left the office she saw no one. She returned to her apartment on the Calle de la Magdalena each night after work and busied herself packing, though there was not too much of it to do. Other than some new clothes, she had accumulated very little during her year and a half in Madrid. A few books, paintings, some linens. A bracelet heavy with gold charms.

And memories to last her a lifetime.

Often, on those cool autumn nights, she wondered if she had after all been a fool to let Alejandro go. Perhaps she could have done as Doña Inez had advised, what even Alejandro would have accepted—married him and then tried to solve their problems. But she knew, even as she reached for the phone, that problems had to be solved before people married, not afterward.

No matter how much she loved Alejandro, she could

never learn to cope with her fear when he was in the bullring. She could never be like the woman in his painting. She did not have the temperament to be a meek-mannered Spanish wife, never voicing an opinion, content to sit in the background of Alejandro's life.

She knew in her heart she had been right to break it off, but that did not stop the terrible grief that threatened to engulf her on cold, lonely nights.

Esteban was released from the hospital and he and Pepita, at Alejandro's insistence, moved into La Esperanza, where they would stay while Esteban recuperated.

Pepita phoned several times a week to report on Esteban's progress. Alejandro and Rufino were busy at the ranch, she said, and Alejandro was training for his South American tour. He would have one fight in Madrid before he left. Rafa was fine. He and Doña Inez asked every day when she, April, was coming for a visit. Although Pepita did not come right out and ask, April knew the woman was curious about what had happened between her and Alejandro.

Then, in the first week in November, Pepita phoned her at the office and said, "We've decided to be married here at La Esperanza this weekend!"

"Pep, that's wonderful!"

"You've got to come, April. You're my maid of honor."

April's hand tightened on the phone. But before she could speak, Pepita said, "It wouldn't be a proper wedding without you. Please, April. Whatever the problem is between you and Alejandro, it doesn't have anything to do with our friendship. Esteban and I both want you with us when we're married."

"Then I'll come, of course."

"Can you come Friday morning? I've picked out the dresses. They're lacy and flouncy and kind of Gypsyish. You'll love them."

April smiled into the phone. It was good, after the near-tragedy, to hear Pepita so full of joy. So she had said yes, that she would fly in to Cádiz Friday morning. The wedding would be Saturday at noon.

The week passed all too swiftly. She finished packing for her return to New York and did some last-minute gift-shopping for relatives at home and for a wedding present for Pepita and Esteban, finally settling on a silver punch bowl and twelve silver cups.

And because this would be her last weekend outing in Spain, she splurged on a travel suit of dove-gray wool. It was severely tailored but trimmed with a deep silvery-blue fox collar and cuffs. It was elegant and expensive, and when April took a last glance in the mirror before she left on Friday morning, she knew she looked good.

She could not help feeling disappointment when she stepped off the plane to see that Pepita was alone, that Alejandro had not come to meet her.

They went directly to the dressmaker to try on their dresses. April was not sure whether she looked more like Scarlet O'Hara or Bette Davis playing Jezebel in her dress, but she did not voice her feelings to Pepita.

"We'll scatter little pink flowers in your hair," Pepita said. "You'll be beautiful."

"So will you," April said. "You'll knock their socks off."

"What?" Pepita looked blank and April said, "It's an American expression. It means you're going to look sensational." She hugged her friend. "Nervous?"

"No. I can't wait. I'll probably tap my foot all

through the ceremony and tell the *padre* to hurry and get on with it. I'm an impossible woman, April. I'm headstrong and foolish, but oh, I do love Esteban and I'm going to be a good wife. I'll work in the fields and plant his grapes . . ."

April laughed. "I don't think he expects you to do that."

"But I want to. I want to do everything with him. I want to be everything to him. You don't know how it is to love somebody this way."

April, pretending to study the hem of her bridesmaid's dress, had to look away. Perhaps I don't, she thought. Perhaps I don't.

There was a small family party that night at La Esperanza. Doña Inez, looking as regal as a queen in a black silk dress and with diamonds in her ears, sat at the head of the table, flanked by April and Alejandro. Carlos was there, along with Rafa and his brother, Manuel, and Manuel's wife, who had come from Ciudad Real, and Rufino Briviesca, who looked ten years younger than when April had last seen him.

The dining room was festive with flowers and candlelight. Toast after toast was drunk to the bride and groom. Esteban, still looking pale, drank very little. He held Pepita's hand most of the evening, his face full of love, smiling and nodding each time she asked him if he felt all right or if he was tired.

April was grateful for the rapid flow of Rafa's conversation. For Rafa, on the other side of her, was full of questions.

"When do you leave for the United States? Why do you have to go? What's New York like? Don't you like Spain? Why can't you live here at La Esperanza with Uncle Alec and me?"

"That's enough," Alejandro cut in. "Give April a chance to eat."

"But there's so much I want to know," Rafa said. "Is New York a lot larger than Madrid? I know the buildings are taller, but—"

"Why don't you come and see for yourself?" April asked.

"What? You mean come to New York?"

She nodded. "Perhaps you can come next summer."

"Really? Really, April?" His face broke into a smile. "I could visit you in New York?"

"And California," she said.

The boy, his face flushed with excitement, turned to Alejandro. "May I, Uncle Alec? May I visit April?"

"Not in the summer," Alejandro said.

"But—"

"*Matadors* fight in the summer. Or had you forgotten?"

"I . . . yes, I guess I had. But I go to school in the winter." He chewed his lower lip as he glanced from his uncle to April.

"What about Easter vacation?" April persisted.

"That's during *Semana Santa,* Holy Week. There are always bullfight fiestas right after that." Rafa's eyes looked strangely bleak.

"Well . . ." April hesitated. "Whenever you can, Rafa. Perhaps when you're through high school."

"That's two years from now. You'll probably be married by then and your husband won't want me around."

"That's enough!" Alejandro's face was stiff with anger. "Let's hear no more about this. You're behaving like a child."

The boy's face turned scarlet. He glanced quickly at his uncle, then down at his plate.

"We'll work something out," April said, trying to ease Rafa's embarrassment. "There must be some season of the year when the bullrings close, even in Spain. And who knows, Rafa, in a year or two you might decide to try something else. Something besides the bulls, I mean. You might want to be a lawyer or an engineer, an airline pilot or even an astronaut."

"I've thought about being a pilot. Maybe I'll do that when I'm forty. I mean after I retire from being a *matador*."

"Forty!" April smiled at him. "You'd have to start lots sooner than that, Rafa. You'd have to take special courses at the university. Things like math and physics."

"It's late, Rafael," Alejandro cut in. "Time for you to go to bed."

"But tonight's special, Uncle Alec. I thought—"

"Please say your good nights."

"But I haven't had my dessert."

"Neither have I," Doña Inez said. "And I'm really very tired, Rafa. Perhaps you wouldn't mind going to the kitchen and getting two desserts. We can eat them in my room and chat for a few minutes."

She avoided looking at Alejandro and instead said to April, "Why don't you join me for breakfast tomorrow morning, dear? It will give us a chance for a visit before all the excitement begins. Is eight-thirty all right?"

"Yes, Doña Inez. And thank you. I'd like to have breakfast with you."

"Then I'll expect you." She went around the table to embrace Pepita and Esteban. "All of us wish you happiness," she said. Then, still ignoring Alejandro, she turned back to Rafa and said, "I'll see you in a few minutes, *muchacho*."

The rest of them finished the meal in silence. And

when they were through, Pepita and Esteban excused themselves to walk in the garden. One by one the others drifted off until only Alejandro and April were left at the table.

He looked at her, then carefully folded his napkin and put it on the table. "Rafa is only a boy, April. He's young and impressionable. And he's fond of you."

"I'm fond of him too."

"He's going to miss you when you leave." He poured a splash of wine in his glass. Then, his eyes smoldering with anger, he said, "It isn't good for him to hope for things he can't have."

"Things he can't have?" April's voice was icy. "Like a trip to America to visit me? Like a career that might be more to his choosing?"

"That's not fair! Rafa chose to become a *matador*."

"Because he wants to be like you."

"That's not the reason."

"Because he'd do anything for you. He'd be anything you want him to be."

"I'd never make Rafa do anything he didn't want to do."

"Wouldn't you?" April's hands tightened in her lap, and in a voice that shook with intensity she said, "Don't you see, Alec? Rafa would do anything to make you proud of him, and you are proud of him, I know that. But there's something else too. I think when you look at Rafa you see yourself when you were fourteen. It's—it's like a part of you will go on forever. By the time you're ready to retire, Rafa will be at the height of his career and it will almost be like you're doing the same thing twice."

"That's ridiculous!" His voice shook with anger.

"Don't you care that he could be hurt or crippled?

That he could be killed? My God, Alejandro, aren't you ever afraid for him?"

Suddenly he pushed his chair back, and before April knew what he was going to do, he had yanked her to her feet. *"Afraid?"* His eyes narrowed with fury. "Goddamnit, you don't even know the meaning of the word!"

"Don't I? How do you think I feel when you're in the ring? But you don't care about that, do you? You don't care about Rafa or—"

He grabbed her shoulders and shook her. "Not care about Rafa? Damn you! Don't you know that every time he's in the ring a part of me is so paralyzed with fear that I can scarcely breathe?" His hands tightened on her shoulders. "Damn you to hell, *gringa!* You *don't* know! You don't know how it feels when a bull lowers his head to charge, when his horns reach out for your face or your stomach. You don't know."

"Then why do you fight?" she said in a choked voice. "Why do you let Rafa fight?"

He stared at her, searching her face. Then, as abruptly as he had grabbed her, he let her go, and with a deep, shattering breath he said, "I couldn't make you understand, April. Not in a hundred years."

"Because I'm an American?"

"That's right, because you're an American." He rubbed a hand across his face and said, in a voice that sounded infinitely weary, "I'm sorry I yelled at you, April. It's late and I'm—I'm tired."

She wanted to reach out to him then, wanted to hold him and comfort him, wanted to sooth the look of bleakness from his face and tell him that she loved him. She wanted to say, "Be whatever you want to be, my darling. I will still love you."

She wanted to, but she couldn't.

Later that night, because she could not sleep, April stood for a long time in front of the French doors of the room that Alejandro had redecorated for her and looked down into the patio to watch the gentle play of water in the fountain.

When a figure emerged from the shadows, she saw that it was Alejandro. He put a foot up on the fountain and stood for a long time looking out toward the distant mountains. After a little while he began to walk toward the fields, in the direction of the bullring.

Again, as she had earlier, April wanted to reach out to him. Wanted to run after him and tell him that she loved him and that, after all, was all that mattered.

Wanted to, but didn't.

A table had been placed in front of the windows of Doña Inez's bedroom. It was set with fine bone china and gleaming silver pots of hot coffee and boiled milk. A red rose and a pink rose were in a porcelain vase.

"I rather think the roses are from Alejandro," Doña Inez said. "He knew I was furious with him last night."

"Yes, so was I." April bent to kiss the old lady's cheek.

"He loves Rafa, you know."

"I know. He told me last night that it's because I'm an American that I don't understand bullfighting."

"Nonsense! I'm Spanish and I don't understand it. I've seen Alejandro fight only twice, the day he made his debut in Madrid and the day he fought in Segovia with Rafa."

"But I thought Spanish women . . . Alejandro said Spanish women . . ."

"Don't you believe him. Be she Spanish or American, mother, grandmother, sister or wife, if a woman loves a man, she's going to be sick with terror each time he goes into the ring. Alejandro's mother never saw him fight, and until the day she died she begged him to quit." She reached over and patted April's hand. "You can't help the way you feel, my dear, any more than I can. We both love Alejandro. I just wish it could have been different between you because I would have loved to have had you for a granddaughter. You would have brought great joy to all of us."

She looked out of the window and then, with a resolute smile on her face, turned back to April and said, "Now let's eat, shall we? The wedding is in less than three hours."

A bright Andalusian sun shone down upon them that day as they gathered on the patio to witness the wedding.

Pepita had never looked so lovely. Her black hair was drawn back from her face. A tall tortoiseshell comb held her veil in place. Her white off-the-shoulder gown fitted snugly at her waist and fell in ruffled flounces to the tops of her white satin shoes. The only touch of color was the small beribboned bouquet of violets that she carried.

Esteban, standing next to the flower-decked fountain, waited beside Alejandro, while first April—dressed in pink, with blossoms of pink wood sorrels scattered in her auburn hair—then Pepita, came to stand beside the fountain.

The old familiar words were spoken simply and beautifully.

"Do you take this woman? Do you promise to love and honor her? To cleave only on to her?"

April was intensely aware of Alejandro, and though she tried not to, her gaze went to his face. His eyes met hers, Gypsy eyes that were filled with longing and confusion.

The voice of the priest mingled with the song of a bird. A yellow butterfly hovered near the fountain as Pepita turned to hand her bouquet of violets to April. Her dark eyes were solemn as she held out her left hand to receive Esteban's ring.

"I promise," she said.

"I promise," he said, as with tender hands he lifted the white lace veil and touched his lips to Pepita's.

It was over. Everyone applauded and gathered to congratulate the happy couple. April kissed Pepita, then Esteban. She smiled and said all the right things. And tried not to look at Alejandro.

Corks popped from bottles of champagne, toasts were drunk, musicians played. Finally lunch was served at a long table set up at one side of the patio.

"Where are you going for your honeymoon?" Manuel's wife asked Pepita.

"To Marbella. We've rented a house on the beach for a month. It will be good for Esteban to rest before we settle into the house we're redoing at the vineyard."

"So he's going to make a country girl out of you," Carlos said with a smile.

"But I've promised her a month in Madrid every summer," Esteban said. "She can shop and go to the theatre and—"

"Who will take care of the babies? Six children need a lot of care."

"Only six?" Esteban pretended disappointment. "I could have sworn you promised me ten."

"How many children are you going to have, April?" Rafa asked.

April's face flushed but she managed a smile and

said, "I'd have a dozen if I thought they'd all be as nice as you." Then, linking her arm in his, she said, "Come and dance with me."

They had only danced a few minutes when Alejandro tapped Rafa on the shoulder and said, "My turn. Sorry." And when the boy released her, Alejandro drew April into his arms.

April's body sighed against his. Perhaps it was the champagne, perhaps it was because after this day it would all be over. But whatever the reason, she felt the tension ease out of her as she gave herself up to his arms.

"I've never seen you look so lovely." Alejandro reached to touch her hair, and in a voice so low she could barely hear him said, "I'll never forget you, April."

"Nor I you, Alejandro."

He rested his face against her hair. "I'm sorry if I shouted at you last night. Please believe me when I tell you that I would never do anything to hurt Rafa. I couldn't love him more if he were my own son."

"I know."

"I said what I did because I—I don't want him to become too attached to you. You're leaving Spain. You may never return. It's bad enough for me, April. I don't want Rafa to suffer too."

"Alec, please . . ." Hot tears stung her eyes.

"I'm sorry." He danced her away from the others to a place where they were hidden by a bower of autumn flowers. "The best man hasn't kissed the maid of honor," he said in a husky voice.

April lifted her face to his for a kiss that was curiously gentle and remote, a kiss that said good-bye instead of hello.

It was late in the afternoon when Pepita whispered, "Help me change, April. We're going to leave in a little while."

And when she had changed into a red wool suit, she looked at herself in the mirror. "I can only be demure so long," she said with a grin. "Then the Pepita in me has to come out. Do I look all right?"

"You look radiant, Señora Davalos."

"Señora Davalos." Impulsively she hugged April. "I'm so happy. So much happier than I deserve to be. Oh, April, if I had lost Esteban . . ."

"But you didn't, Pepita. You didn't."

"I wish that you and Alejandro—"

"No, please don't say anything."

"But I want you to be happy. You and Alejandro belong together. He's crazy in love with you."

"I don't want to discuss it, Pepita."

"But don't you see, April. You're doing the same thing I did. You're refusing to marry Alejandro because you don't like what he does."

"No! It's not the same! Esteban only wanted to farm. That's not the same thing at all."

"Isn't it?" Pepita clasped April's hands in hers. "We both fell in love with a man because that man was different from anyone else we'd ever known. Then we tried to change him. I tried to change Esteban and I almost lost him. You're doing the same thing with Alejandro."

"No, there's a difference."

"Don't let him walk out of your life, April. Accept him the way he is. Love him the way he is."

April tried to fight the tears that spilled. And when she could not, she covered her face with her hands and whispered, "I can't, Pepita. I just can't."

* * *

Quite early the next morning April got up and dressed. The house was quiet after the uproar of the day before, and it seemed strange to walk through the now silent corridors. All that remained of the wedding and the reception that followed were pieces of colored paper streamers and wilted flowers and the crunch of rice under her feet as she crossed the patio.

When a maid offered her a cup of coffee, she refused and, leaving the patio, walked down through the fields, still damp with morning dew, in the direction of the bullring.

There was a hush about everything this morning, and except for a covey of quail that flew protesting from a clump of bushes as she passed, there was only stillness.

With a sigh April rested her arms on the top of the fence that circled the bullring. It seemed to her in that quiet moment as though she could almost hear the rush of hooves against the dirt and the snap of the cape.

What made men fight? she wondered. What was it about the profession that called to them, that got in their blood so that they cared for nothing else, lived only for that moment when they stepped out of the shadows and into the sun? What magic, what devils, made them flirt with death?

"A *peseta* for your thoughts."

April turned quickly. She hadn't heard Alejandro come up behind her. "I was thinking about the bulls," she said.

He turned away from the ring to look out over the fields, golden in the autumn sun, and at the rise of mountains in the distance. "I've thought about what you said the other night, April, and I'm going to talk to

Rafa. I won't discourage him from a career in the ring, but I am going to make it clear that I want the decision to be his. I want him to be his own man, to make his own decisions." He smiled his wry smile. "And I'll try to arrange a time when he can visit you. I suppose every boy should see New York and California—at least once."

April had to wait a moment before she could speak. When she did, she managed to keep her voice light. "I'll take good care of him and send him back safely to you."

"I know you will."

"Well . . ." She glanced at her watch. "My plane leaves at eleven-thirty. I guess I'd better get back to the house. I just wanted one more look. La Esperanza is a lovely place, Alejandro."

"It will be a good place to come when I retire, April. I really will make it the best brave-bull ranch in Spain then." He looked at her for a long moment, then reached out to touch her face. "April. I still think it's a strange name. What did I say once? That April was a month and not a woman. That it was springtime and—"

"And the promise of summer," she said in a husky voice.

"But that was a long time ago, wasn't it? Summer has gone. Winter is coming."

They didn't speak for a long moment, and then Alejandro said, "When do you leave Spain?"

"On the twentieth."

"I'm fighting in Madrid on the twelfth. I hope you'll come."

"I'm going to be awfully busy, Alejandro."

"Try to make time. This will be the last *corrida* you'll

ever have to sit through. We can have dinner at Botin's afterward."

"All right." April tried to smile. "It's a date, then."

He took her hand and looked down into her eyes. Then he led her back through the golden fields of La Esperanza.

Chapter 18

APRIL SPENT MOST OF THE WEEK AFTER HER RETURN FROM La Esperanza packing, unpacking and repacking. She paced the small elegant apartment on the Calle de la Magdalena, staring at the now empty bookshelves, the naked walls and the cartons of boxes, ready to be shipped to New York.

It was strange, she thought as she packed, that she had not felt this sadness when she left her home in Napa Valley to go away to school or when she had closed her apartment in New York to come to Spain. Never before had she experienced this terrible emptiness, this feeling that she would soon leave everything and everyone dear to her.

One afternoon, frantic with indecision, April left her apartment and walked aimlessly through the streets of Madrid. Or perhaps she only told herself that she walked aimlessly, because suddenly she found herself in front of Alejandro's apartment.

Noiselessly April let herself into the silent apartment. The air was still with the closed-up musty smell of emptiness. She looked around the large living room, at the sofa where she had seen Alejandro surrounded by girls, at the bullfight posters above the bar. She went to stand by the sliding glass doors that opened out onto the balcony and remembered how the lights of the city had looked that night.

Finally, because it was why she had come, she went into the bedroom to see the painting.

The drapes were drawn, the room was dark. She stood for a moment in the center of the room as a flood of memories came back to her: of the first time Alejandro had kissed her; of other times. The feel of the fur spread against her naked body. The touch of his lips against her skin.

Finally, with a sigh, she opened the drapes and let the afternoon sunshine flood the room.

Then she looked at the painting. At the woman depicted in "The Matador's Wife."

She studied the pale skin, the dark eyes that gazed so sadly at the jacket she mended. The light filtering in from the narrow window in the painting was scarcely adequate for the woman to see by, nor was the small flicker of flame from the votive candle beside her. Why did she strain so to see? Why didn't she wait until morning?

Because she *has* to have something to do, April thought. She has to keep her hands busy or she'll go mad. She must love him—*her* matador—to be able to live with such pain.

April sat with the woman until the afternoon shadows darkened the room. When she left she knew what it was that she would do.

The high, thin notes of the *clarín,* clear and sharp and shrill, split through the November air. Overhead the clouds were dark with the threat of rain. And as the last note of the horn died away, a growl of thunder was heard.

The *alguacil*, dressed in his black velvet costume and mounted on a pure white horse, rode majestically into the ring. He approached the authority's box and doffed his plumed hat to ask for permission to begin the spectacle, and the music began.

From her seat in the first row above the place where the matadors would stand, April looked toward the *puerta de cuadrillas*, the door through which the three matadors would pass. She sat erect, gloved hands folded in her lap, forcing herself to appear composed.

She had taken great pains dressing that day. Because the temperature was in the low sixties—and she knew it would be cooler by nightfall—she decided to wear the gray suit with the silver-blue fox collar and a hat of matching fur she'd found in a shop on the Gran Vía. Her cinnamon eyes were outlined a bit more than was usual for her, and she had accentuated their color with a smudge of pale turquoise eye shadow to make them look even larger. On her lips she wore a new shade of lipstick called Autumn Leaves.

The only jewelry she wore was the gold charm bracelet Alejandro had given her.

Heads turned when April got out of the taxi at the bullring. Eyes followed her into the entrance and down to her seat. But she paid no attention to them; her eyes were on the bullring.

Alejandro had phoned at noon to say that her ticket had been delivered to the doorman of her apartment.

"Carlos will wait for you after the fight," he had told her. "He'll take you back to the apartment. I've made reservations at Botin's for eight o'clock. That will give us a chance to have a drink before we go."

"All right, Alejandro."

"The bulls look good today, April."

"I'm glad."

"It's going to be cool. There may be a storm later. Dress warmly."

"I will."

"Then I'll see you later?"

"Yes, darling." She had heard the small intake of his breath at her use of the word.

The *clarín* sounded again. There was an expectant hush. Then the beautiful strains of *Cielo Andaluz* filled the stands. The *alguacil*, now standing in front of the matadors who were waiting for him to lead them into the arena, started forward. Behind him came the matadors, the *banderilleros*, the picadors mounted on their blindfolded horses, the *monosabios* who would help the picadors, clean the ring and handle the mules that would pull the dead bulls from the ring.

How handsome Alejandro is, April thought, remembering the first time she had seen him. He'd been wearing a black suit of lights that day, and the satin had clung to him like a second skin. Even then, she thought now, she had felt a surge of emotion when she looked at him, a quickening of her heart and, yes, a prickle of desire that had amused and frightened her.

Today his suit of lights was almost the same shade as his green Gypsy eyes.

The parade of matadors crossed the golden sand to the other side of the arena and stopped just below where April sat. Alejandro slid his *capote de paseo,* the beautifully embroidered cape that he had over his left shoulder, onto the railing in front of April. Their eyes met for a moment before he turned back to the arena.

His was the second bull. It was a fair animal and

Alejandro fought well. But the sword was not good and it took him three tries before he was able to kill.

The third matador had better luck. He fought well, killed with the first sword thrust and was awarded an ear. The next matador allowed too many pics. As all the *aficionados* knew, it was the matador who controlled the pics. A brave matador will allow only enough of a pic to slow the animal so that he can be played properly. But if a matador is afraid of an animal, he will allow him to be weakened until he is no longer dangerous.

The *faena* was a disaster. The crowd was mad at the matador for ruining a good bull, and the matador was mad at the crowd for whistling at him.

Alejandro's second animal was big and black, with a wide set of almost perfect horns. He did several beautifully classic *verónicas* and ended the series with a *media-verónica*. When it was time for the picadors he watched them carefully and signaled immediately when he knew that one pic was enough.

When he indicated that he would plant the *banderillas,* the arena rang with applause. He cited the bull, arched his back, then raised himself on his toes, the colorful sticks held high above his head. When the bull charged, Alejandro ran in a quarter circle toward him, then cut in across the charge, and as the bull lowered his head Alejandro brought his feet together, raised the colored sticks high and plunged them into the hump of neck muscle, dancing away as the long white horns reached out for him.

When it was time for the *faena*, he dedicated it to the crowd and received a scattering of applause. He began with a spectacular *pase del pendulo* in the center of the ring; then, without moving, a *pase del desdén;* then *naturales* that flowed into a *pase de pecho*. On and on, calm and sure of himself, close and still closer to the bull, moving with agonizing slowness as the horns grazed his body.

His performance was artistically beautiful. The crowd knew it and April knew it in spite of the nails she dug into her palms or the sweat that beaded her upper lip. Alejandro was magnificent. This was where he belonged. This was what he was meant to do.

He made pass after beautiful pass as the band played and the people cheered him on. When it was time to kill, there was a moment of quiet as collectively the thousands of spectators held their breaths for this final moment of truth.

Alejandro stood poised, the *muleta* furled clockwise over the stick in his left hand, the sword in his right. Slowly he moved the red cloth to fix the bull's attention. Then, as the animal lowered his head, Alejandro went forward over the horns, horns that reached for his body even as he moved to slide against the animal's flanks.

As the animal staggered and fell, the arena erupted into shouts of *"Torero! Torero! Torero!"*

He came back to the *barrera*. Carlos handed him a dipper of water and he took a sip of it and then rinsed his mouth. Then he took a towel and wiped his face.

The *aguacil* stood before the authority, and when the authority nodded, the *aguacil* handed the trophies to Alejandro and embraced him, then stepped back as Alejandro began his tour of the ring.

It was as it had been that first day. The crowd threw him *botas* of wine, and because it was his last bull of the day, he drank from several of them, his head back, his strong throat working as he shot the fine stream of wine into his mouth. Hats and bouquets of red roses sailed into the ring. A high-heeled pump, a man's shoe, a shower of carnations.

He was almost at the end of the circle, and when he came closer, April stood with the people around her, applauding as they applauded, smiling down at him when he looked up at her.

Then, as she had done that first time, she pulled her hat off and threw it into the ring.

For a moment it seemed that he was too surprised to catch it. But he did, holding it aloft for a moment while the crowd strained to see who had thrown a silver-fox hat and waited for him to throw it back.

But as he had done that very first time, he looked up at her and smiled that wry smile of his before he turned to walk to the middle of the ring, the hat still clutched in his hand, to take his final bow.

Chapter 19

WHEN APRIL STEPPED OFF THE ELEVATOR WITH CARLOS, she could hear the music coming from Alejandro's apartment. Carlos raised his eyebrows and said, "I was afraid of that. Fans, friends and hangers-on. They're hard to discourage, April."

"Yes, I suppose they are."

"Alec will escape as soon as he can. You're going to dinner at Botin's?"

April nodded. "Won't you join us?"

"No, but thanks. I've got a lot of last-minute arrangements to make for the South American tour and I have to be up early tomorrow." He hesitated. "I know you and I got off to a bad start, but I like to think we're friends now, April. I wish you were coming with us."

"So do I," she said with a slight smile as he opened the apartment door and ushered her inside.

It was just as it had been that first time: one huge overcrowded, smoke-filled cocktail party.

"Alec's probably still dressing," Carlos shouted over the noise. "Can I get you a drink?"

"A sherry, please."

He took her hand and led her through the throng of people. Just as they reached the bar, they saw Alejandro emerge from his bedroom. In gray flannel slacks, a gray turtleneck sweater and a navy cashmere jacket, his black hair still damp from the shower, he looked as handsome as April had ever seen him.

When he saw her he hurried to her side and, with a frown, said, "I didn't invite these people, April. They just came. I'm sorry."

"It's all right, Alejandro. I understand."

"We'll break away in a little while."

"You were very good today."

"I had good luck with the second bull."

She shook her head. "You were very good," she said again.

There was a puzzled look in his eyes, but before he could speak, there was a loud squeal and April turned to see a small dark-haired woman waving a bejeweled hand.

"Alec! Darling!" The voice rose to a coloratura pitch as the woman started toward them, a large alligator purse held in front of her like a battering ram.

"Oh, Christ," Alejandro said under his breath. "Carlos, can you—?"

But before he could finish, the woman flung herself into his arms. "Darling! Darling, darling, darling!" she cried, then planted a moist openmouthed kiss on his lips.

"Gabby," Alejandro said, trying to extricate himself. "This is a . . . a surprise. I thought you were still in Portofino." He took her arms from around his neck and stepped back.

"I was sick of Portofino, *mi amor.*" With an impatient hand she pushed her mane of dark hair back from her face—a face, April noted, that was a flawless pale ivory, with thin black brows and long artificial lashes that accentuated her large black eyes. The slash of bright lipstick was vivid against the pale skin.

With a tinkling crescendo of a laugh she captured Alejandro's hand. "I longed for Madrid and, yes, I longed for you. You can't imagine how I missed you, *adorado*."

"Gabby . . ." Alejandro tried to smile, but there was a line of tension around his lips. "Uh, you know Carlos, don't you? And this is April. April Juneau."

"French?" Gabby said with a lift of her brow.

"*Gringa*," April said.

"*Gringa?* How odd you'd use that word."

"But it's what I am."

The wide eyes narrowed in speculation. "You're visiting Madrid?"

"Not exactly."

"And you're a friend of Alejandro's?"

"Not exactly."

The red mouth pursed peevishly. "Not a friend?"

"No, I wouldn't call me that." April linked an arm through Alejandro's and smiled up at him. "I'm Alejandro's fiancée."

The other woman's gasp was audible. The dark eyes went wide with surprise. But before she could speak, April said, "You will excuse us, won't you? We're leaving for South America on Friday and we have a million things to do. Carlos, would you fix the *señorita* a drink? Alec and I have reservations for dinner and I'm afraid we really must run."

She looked up at Alejandro and, with an innocently sweet smile, said, "Let's say good night to our guests, darling. Carlos will take good care of Gabby. And if he doesn't, I'm sure there are others who will."

The muscles of Alejandro's arm tensed under her

fingers. But with a smile that bordered somewhere between amused and dangerous, he allowed her to lead him through the throng of people to the door.

"I didn't know you could be so protective," he said when they were in the elevator.

"Didn't you, *darling?*"

He winced. "Could you use a different word?"

"Of course. How about *mi amor?* Or *precioso?*"

His hand flashed out and gave her an ungentlemanly swat.

"Ouch!" April cried, just as the elevator doors opened to allow an elderly couple to enter.

She and Alejandro didn't speak as the elevator doors opened on the ground floor or when they were in the taxi, but once they were seated at Botin's he said, "Now what was that all about, April? Just a little female jealousy—or something else?"

She put the menu down and looked across the table at him. "Something else," she said as the waiter arrived.

"We'd like a bottle of wine now," Alejandro told him. "We'll order in a few minutes."

After the wine had been poured and the waiter had turned away, Alejandro said, "All right, April. What is it?"

She hesitated for a moment as she studied his face. He had been wrong about her reaction to Gabby; she was not jealous of the woman. If anything she was amused. For the first time in her life she was completely sure of what she was doing. She had thought it out carefully and knew that she had made a decision that was right for her and for Alejandro.

She picked up the glass and took a sip of the wine. "You said once that you wanted to live with me, Alejandro."

"I still do."

"Before . . . before we ever discussed marriage, you asked me to go to South America with you."

"That seems like a long time ago now."

"Does it?" She toyed with her glass. "You know, Alec, through all of this—the problems and the disagreements—I've never stopped loving you."

He waited, his green eyes intent on hers.

"For a while I tried not to—love you, I mean. Because I was so afraid when you were in the ring."

He reached across the table and took her hand.

"When you first asked me to marry you, I said no."

"And now?"

April smiled at him. "I've canceled my flight back to the States, Alec. If you still want me to, I'll go with you to South America."

"April!" There was a wonderful light in his eyes, and when he spoke—when he said, "Of course I want you with me"—his voice was husky with emotion. "We can be married before we leave. It will take a bit of doing, but—"

"Alec." April looked down into the wine and slowly twisted the glass. "I want to be with you," she said, not looking at him. "But I don't want to marry you."

"What? What in the hell are you talking about?" He raised his voice and the people at the next table turned to stare at them. "Are you trying to say that you'll travel with me—that you'll live with me—but that you won't marry me? That doesn't make sense, April. Not now. Not the way we feel about each other."

"It does make sense, Alejandro." Gently she freed her hand and, with a bright smile, said, "There's an old saying, isn't there, about mistresses being more fun than wives? We'll have fun, Alec. I'll be the best companion you've ever had. No one will ever love you as much as I do, darling, and . . ."

His dark brows drew together as April went on. He didn't interrupt her but watched her face as she spoke.

With a growing sense of discomfort, a feeling that this was not going the way she had planned, April found that she was unable to stop talking. She'd never been to South America, she said. What fun it would be to travel together. Could they see Cuzco and Machu Picchu?

Alejandro nodded, smiling a strange bitter smile as his Gypsy eyes grew darker and darker.

"It will be such fun, Alec. Where will we spend Christmas? Can we spend it in Rio? Or perhaps Mexico City? I've heard that Mexico City is beautiful during the holidays."

And with a laugh that didn't quite come off, she said, "Just think of all the charms I'll have when we return."

"Not just charms," he said in an oddly tight voice. "Emeralds from Columbia, furs from Peru. Those are the kinds of presents men give their mistresses, April."

Before she could answer, he signaled to the waiter, then asked in a carefully pleasant voice what she would like.

"*Entremeses* to begin? Navarra trout? That's always excellent. And the roast lamb, I think."

The waiter hovered to fill their wineglasses and to set out some twenty small dishes of the *entremeses* Alejandro had ordered. But Alejandro waved him away when the man tried to serve, and he picked out the choicest appetizers for April's plate.

He carried the conversation throughout the dinner, and all the while a white line of anger grew rigid and set around his mouth.

April tried to eat, but it was difficult to swallow.
Even the wine stuck in her throat. She saw the hardness
of Alejandro's jaw, the glint of his eyes.

When he ordered fresh strawberry parfaits for
dessert, she said, "No, thank you. I—I can't really."

"Then shall we go?" And when she nodded, he came
around to her side of the table to help her into her
jacket.

There were spatters of rain, and a wind that threatened a downpour, when they stepped out of the
restaurant. Alejandro signaled a taxi, and when they
were inside, April said, "I'd like to go back to my
place."

"Nonsense."

"Alejandro, really, I—"

He gave the driver his address as though he hadn't
heard her. Then, turning to her, he said, "You're all
packed?"

"Yes."

"Good. We leave Friday morning. We can leave your
things in my apartment until we return to Madrid.
Then, if our . . . arrangement has worked out, we'll
find you a suitable place. It won't be necessary for you
to work, of course. I'm quite able to pay all of your
expenses."

April's hands clenched in helpless rage: rage at
Alejandro because he was so coldly, so arrogantly, sure
of himself; rage at herself because she'd brought this
on.

When he let her into the apartment, he said, "Make
me a drink, will you? Cognac, please."

Back straight, legs stiff, April walked to the bar.

Alejandro hung the navy cashmere jacket over a
chair and sprawled on the sofa when she handed him

the drink. "This place is a mess," he said looking around him. "It smells like one giant ashtray. You wouldn't mind cleaning up a bit, would you?"

"Of course not." April's voice was steely cold as she snatched a tray off the bar and, with a great deal of clashing and banging, gathered up empty glasses and foul-smelling ashtrays and carried them into the kitchen. Then, without even glancing at Alejandro, she marched into the bedroom, grabbed her fur hat off the bed and marched back out.

"Don't bother to get up," she snapped as she headed for the door.

"Where do you think you're going?"

"I'm going home!"

"Not until we discuss a few things."

"There's nothing to discuss."

"The hell there isn't!" His angry green eyes blazed into hers as unceremoniously he took her arm and propelled her across the room to a chair.

He sat down facing her, and after a moment he said, "You've proposed being my mistress, so there are things we need to talk about: the kind of apartment you'd expect, the kind of car, a clothes allowance. Whether or not you expect me to be faithful. I might decide to marry, but that need not interfere with our arrangement. I would, however, expect you to be faithful for the time we're together."

"The time we're together!" Hot color rose in her cheeks. "What do you think I am?"

"We already know that, don't we, April?"

Her eyes went wide with shock. Then, before she could stop herself, she was out of the chair, her hand slashing out, catching him a stinging blow across his face.

"You bastard!" Tears of anger and humiliation filled

her eyes. "Bastard!" She drew back to hit him again, but he caught her hand in midair.

"Don't try that again," he said in a deadly voice. His hand tightened on her wrist, forcing her back into the chair.

Trembling in anger, sick with reaction, April stared at him. She was unable to believe that this was the man who had once said he loved her, the man who had asked her to marry him.

With cold, hard eyes he looked her up and down. Then, in a voice heavy with irony, he shook his head and said, "But I have my doubts about us, April. I'm not sure it would work out. If I decide to take a mistress, I'd want someone who was a little easier to get along with—someone who catered more to my needs, who wouldn't mind if I took a wife so long as she was taken care of. You're too American, too independent, for that."

He reached for his glass and finished the last of the cognac. "So I'm sorry, my dear, but I've decided to refuse your offer. I don't want you to be my mistress. But if you'd like to spend the night . . ."

April could not believe the cruel casualness of his words.

A clap of thunder broke the stillness of the room, jarring her to action. She grabbed her purse off the coffee table and started toward the door.

"I'll get a taxi for you if you wait a moment," Alejandro said.

"I don't want you to get a taxi for me." April's voice shook with rage. "I don't want anything from you." Before he could move to stop her, she ran out the door.

When she stepped outside the building, the slash of wind-driven rain almost blinded her. But it didn't matter. Nothing mattered. She didn't even look for a taxi; she just ran—ran until she was out of breath, high heels tapping against the rain-slick pavement, strands of wet hair plastered to her face.

Finally, gasping for breath, feeling as though she had been wounded, she leaned against the side of a building and cried great racking sobs of grief and humiliation.

And for a love that had somehow turned to hate.

Meanwhile, back in his apartment on the Gran Vía, Alejandro rested his head back against the chair, his eyes closed as he fought the rise of anguish in his throat. Then he got up and went to the bar and poured another cognac. But when he did, he raised his head and looked at himself in the mirror over the bar and, with a cry, picked up the glass and hurled it at his reflection.

Chapter 20

COLD NOVEMBER RAIN SLASHED RELENTLESSLY AGAINST the windows of the apartment on the Calle de la Magdalena. April clutched a blanket to her chin and struggled to a sitting position. She looked at the half-cup of cold tea on the nightstand and wrinkled her nose in distaste. Then with a sigh she shook two aspirin out of a bottle, put them in her mouth and washed them down with the cold tea.

Bleary-eyed, she looked around the bleak bedroom. It was as though she'd already left. All of the pictures were off the walls. Boxes were stacked in a corner. The rugs she had bought in Morocco were rolled and ready for shipping.

The living room was even worse, and the kitchen was barer than Mother Hubbard's cupboard. She'd existed on tea and toast for the last three days and even had difficulty getting that down.

That first morning after the terrible scene with Alejandro, April had awakened with a headache, sore throat, red eyes and a runny nose. She knew that it was her own fault, because she'd walked all the way home from his apartment in the blinding rain. She'd thrown the dove-gray suit, wet fur smelly, over a chair, and crawled in bed without even bothering to dry her hair. The next day her throat was so swollen she could barely speak and she was running a fever.

But all of the discomforts seemed minor compared to the pain and humiliation of the scene with Alejandro. She wept and sniffled for three days, curling her body into a tight ball of misery, covering her face with the blanket to try to blot out the world and the memory of that night.

Now, as April lay with the blanket to her chin, staring hopelessly up at the ceiling, she remembered that the next day was Friday and that Alejandro was leaving for South America. Her hands balled into fists and hot tears streaked her face. As long as she lived she would never forget the scornful way Alejandro had looked at her.

Late that afternoon the rain finally slowed to a steady drizzle and she drifted to sleep. When the phone rang she debated whether or not to answer it; then, because it had always been impossible for her to ignore either a ringing doorbell or a ringing phone, she picked it up and said hello.

"April?" Pepita asked. "April, is that you?"

"Yes," she croaked. "It's more or less me. How are you, Señora Davalos?"

"Wonderful."

"Where are you?"

"At the vineyard. We got back last night. April, are you ill?"

"Just a cold."

"You sound terrible."

"I sound worse than I feel."

"Have you seen a doctor?"

"No, dear. Not necessary. I'll be fine in a day or two. How did you enjoy Marbella?"

"It was paradise. We had a room overlooking the sea. The weather was perfect. Esteban was perfect."

"How's he feeling?"

"Better. He still tires easily, but I make him rest every afternoon. He's tan now and he looks marvelous."

"That's good." April's head began to pound and she pressed her hand against it.

"Have you seen Alejandro?"

"Uh . . . yes. I—I went to the *corrida* last Sunday."

"But did you *see* him? To talk to, I mean."

"We had dinner later."

"And?"

April closed her eyes. "He's leaving tomorrow for South America."

"I see." After a moment's silence Pepita said, "Are you sure you're all right, April."

"Sure I'm sure."

"Call me before you leave for New York."

"Of course." She wanted desperately to end this conversation so she could rest her head.

"Take care of yourself, April."

"You too. Love to Esteban." April put the phone down and closed her eyes, pressing her fingers against her temples to try to force the pain away.

When she awoke the next morning, she was so dizzy she could barely stagger out of bed. But she dragged herself to the bathroom, splashed water on her face and took two aspirin. By the time she started for the kitchen, she was trembling so badly that she knew she had to lie down or fall down. The cup of tea would have to wait.

Her eyes closed against the hammering in her head. She tried to drift back to sleep, but thoughts of Alejandro prodded her awake. Today was Friday. She reached out and put her hand on the phone. In spite of everything, the anger and the hurt, the final dreadful words, she wanted desperately to hear his voice. But slowly she shook her head. There was nothing she could say to Alejandro now. It had all been said.

"Forget him," she whispered into the silence of the room. "Forget that you loved him. Love him. . . ." Finally she drifted into a feverish sleep.

The high sharp notes of the *clarín* sounded. Alejandro, dressed in his black suit of lights, came into the ring. He had a woman on each arm. The crowd applauded. He bowed and the women waved scarlet fingertips. The *clarín* sounded again and he took out a red cape and swirled it, calling first one, then the other, of the women to him, passing them under the cape and around his body, smiling up at the crowd when they shouted, *"Olé, Matador! Olé!"*

The *clarín* again. And again. April stirred, then buried her head in the pillow.

"April!" A voice called to her from a great distance. "April!"

Groggily she struggled to sit up. Someone pounded on her door, ringing the bell again and again.

"All right," she croaked.

Her bare feet were cold. It was hard to walk because the floor tilted. The front door seemed very far away. But she had to reach it, had to open it, so that the pounding would stop.

"Okay," she muttered, "okay, okay," and slid the bolt back.

Alejandro looked at her. "April?" His voice sounded so strange. "April?"

"Go away," she whispered.

Then everything turned black and she slipped down into a long spiraling corridor of nothingness.

Her head against his chest, an arm under her knees.

"Down," she said. "Put me down."

He laid her down on the bed and pulled the blanket over her. She heard the whir of the telephone dial. His voice, calm at first, then demanding as he shouted into the phone.

She felt a cool damp cloth against her face.

"Do you feel better?" he asked.

"Room's tilting." She pressed the cloth against her forehead.

"Does your head hurt?"

"Yes. Oh, yes."

"Have you eaten anything today?"

"What day is today?"

"Friday."

"You're going to South America." She tried to focus on his face, but it was as though she were looking at him through the distorted mirrors of a fun house. The room tilted and spun and she reached out her hand to try to find something to hold on to so she wouldn't fall. Alejandro's hand clasped hers.

A little later a strange man bent over her bed. "How do you feel?" he asked. "Throat hurt?"

"You betcha," April said in English.

"Headache?"

"Buddy Rich in concert."

"What did she say?"

"Yes, she has a headache."

A thermometer under her tongue. Hands opening the neck of her gown to feel her throat. A cold stethoscope against her chest.

"Can you take penicillin, *señorita?* You're not allergic to it?"

"Not allergic."

He moved her onto her side and she felt the sharp prick of a needle.

"She has a fever of almost a hundred and three. Keep her warm. Give her two of these pills every four hours. See that she eats something. I'll be back in the morning."

"Thank you for coming, doctor."

"From the sound of your voice on the phone, I thought I'd better."

April closed her eyes, willing the room to stop its kaleidoscopic spinning. Spinning her to sleep.

A hand on her shoulder roused her. Alejandro said, "You don't have a damn thing in your cupboards or refrigerator. Where the hell do you keep your food?"

"No food," she mumbled. "Going to New York."

A muttered curse. She drifted off again, to be awakened later by the smell of vegetable soup and Alejandro saying, "Wake up, April. I want you to eat something."

Climbing the long way up to a sitting position, she took the spoon in her hand and dipped it in the soup. But when she raised it to her mouth the spoon tipped and the soup dribbled on her gown. "Sorry," she whispered.

"It's all right." Alejandro wiped her chin and the gown with a napkin and began to feed her.

"It's very good," she said politely. "Thank you."

"Would you like some tea?"

"No, thank you. I have to sleep now."

He'd be gone when she awoke, April thought. Or perhaps he'd never been there at all. Perhaps she'd only dreamed him there because she wanted him so badly.

But it wasn't a dream after all. He awoke her later, gave her two pills and helped her drink a cup of tea. He asked her if she had to go to the bathroom, and when she said yes, he helped her out of bed and walked her across the room. But when he tried to go in with her, she clung to the door and said, "Out!"

Four hours later Alejandro awoke her again, shoved more pills at her and fed her a bowl of apple sauce. It was very good and very cool and felt wonderful sliding down her throat.

For the first time that day April felt better, well enough to feel a real distress at the way she looked and to try to smooth her hair back from her face.

"I—I must look awful," she said.

"Not too awful."

"It's very nice of you to—to take care of me, Alejandro. But I'll be all right now. There's no need for you to stay."

"You'd better rest, April. We'll talk later."

"But you don't have to stay, really," she said. And knew that she would die if he left her.

"Lie down." He pulled the blanket up to her chin. "I'll be here if you need anything."

She nodded, turning her face away from him so that he wouldn't see the tears squeezing out of the corners of her eyes. He wasn't going to leave her yet. Not yet.

Sometime later April opened her eyes. It was dark. She stretched, then rolled over, and when she did her body touched his. Startled, not sure that it really was Alejandro, she touched his arm.

"What is it? Are you all right, April?"

"You're . . . you're sleeping with me? You can't!

You're—we're not . . . You'll catch whatever I've got."

"No, I won't." He sat up and switched the light on. "As long as you're awake, you might as well have your pills." He shook them out of the bottle, then supported her back while she drank some water. Then he turned the light off, and before she could object, he lay down beside her.

While she was thinking of all the reasons why he should not be there with her, she fell asleep.

The doctor came the next two mornings, and by the morning of the third day April's temperature was normal. Except when he went out to buy food, Alejandro had not left her side. He fed her, changed her bed and her nightgown and bathed her. He called Pepita to tell her that he was with April and to thank her for telling him that April was ill.

Through it all April had been too sick to object to any of his ministrations. She did not allow herself to wonder why he was here or why he had delayed his trip to South America. She tried not to think of that last terrible scene in his apartment.

Alejandro lay beside her at night, not touching her unless she moved suddenly, when she would feel his hand on her arm and hear his whispered, "What is it? Do you want something?" Once, when she called out during a nightmare, her body trembling from the night horrors that frightened her, he pulled her into his arms and soothed her until she slept.

April knew it had to end, of course. Alejandro was with her because he was a decent man and he felt an obligation because of what they had once had. As soon as she was all right, he would leave her.

When she awoke on the fifth morning he was gone.

Tentatively she called his name. Her voice seemed to reverberate in the empty apartment.

After a long time she got up. She still felt weak, but she took a shower and washed her hair. Then she went into the kitchen and made a cup of tea and took it into the living room.

Perhaps it was better this way, she thought as she sipped the hot tea. They'd said their farewells once before; there was no need to say them again. This way there would be no more tears, no if-only-things-had-been-different words.

The morning lengthened into afternoon. With the coming of twilight, loneliness seeped into the room to cast long shadows of amber gloom.

April lay on the sofa, a blanket over her, her body curled against the bleakness of the room. Finally she drifted into a troubled sleep.

To dream strange and terrible dreams.

Alejandro stood in the middle of a huge bullring, a bullring where the bulls were the spectators instead of people.

The *toril* gate opened. She ran into the ring. She looked around the plaza, then at Alejandro standing in the center of the ring in his black suit of lights.

"Ahaaa, April!" he called to her.

She felt the snap of the cape in her face as he forced her to bend past his body toward the waiting picadors. She looked up in time to see the lance. She screamed, then felt the thrust of pain.

Now Alejandro, smiling his arrogant smile, faced her with colored barbs raised high above his head.

"I'm April!" she cried. "Don't you know me?"

"April's a month," he said, and began his zigzag run toward her.

She tried to run on feet mired in sand as he raised the barbs high above his head. As she screamed a silent scream.

The bullring faded. "Good-bye," Alejandro said. "*Adiós,* farewell, toodleloo. I'm going to South America. It's been nice knowing you, but there's a whole big world out there filled with women who will."

"Who will what?" she asked.

"Who will love me the way I am."

"I love you."

"Do you? Do you? Do You?" And all the while he walked toward a waiting plane.

"Don't go."

"Good-bye."

"Don't go!" Weeping now as she pleaded with him. Even as the door of the plane clicked open. "Oh, please," she wept.

"April?"

"Please don't go."

"April, wake up."

Alejandro sat beside her on the sofa, and without thinking she flung herself into his arms. "I was dreaming," she cried, clinging to him. "You were going away." Then remembering that he was, she shuddered against him, hiding her face in his shoulder, ashamed that he had seen her tears.

"I should have left you a note. But I didn't expect to be gone this long. Did you eat anything?"

"I had some tea."

"Damnit, April!" His arms tightened around her. "You really do need someone to take care of you." He tried to see her face, but she kept it pressed against his shoulder.

He leaned his face against her head. "Your hair smells good."

"I washed it."

"You shouldn't have."

"I dried it right away. I couldn't stand it dirty. I hate dirty hair." Oh, God, she thought, why can't I talk about something beside my hair?

Alejandro put his hands on her shoulders and held her away from him. "We have to talk," he said in a gentle voice.

"I know. I—I know you have to leave, Alejandro. And it's all right. I understand. I appreciate everything you—"

"Be quiet, love." He helped her to sit up and then sat beside her and took her hands. "I want to talk about last Sunday."

April stiffened. "That was a mistake. We both said things we didn't mean."

"I know I did, April. You see, when I saw you at the *corrida* that afternoon, when you threw your hat into the ring the way you'd done that first day, I thought it meant that you had decided to marry me. Then, when you said you wanted to be my mistress, I was hurt. And I wanted to hurt you."

April nodded, her face solemn. "I felt so awful when you . . . when you offered me all those things. I don't want emeralds or furs, Alejandro. That wasn't what I meant when I said what I did. I thought it might be easier for both of us if we just . . . lived together."

He studied her face for a moment. "You were wrong, April. I want you to be my wife, the mother of my children. You were never—from the very first time—just somebody to go to bed with. You were my dear love."

He brushed the hair back from her face. "You *are* my dear love. And now I'm taking over. I'm going to decide what we're going to do and you're going to do it."

"No!" April tried to draw away from him, but he gripped her shoulders and, with a little shake, forced her to look at him.

"I went out this morning because there were things I had to take care of. One of the things I did was call the ranch and talk to grandmother. Then I called Esteban and Pepita. You'll be well enough to travel in two or three days. We're going to fly to the ranch then. I've made arrangements with a priest—"

"A priest?" April's eyes widened in shock.

"—for a priest to marry us next weekend. Grandmother will take care of the details. Rafa's going to be my best man. Pepita will stand up for you and Esteban can give you away."

"You can't just—"

"The day after the wedding we'll fly from Málaga to Bogotá."

"I won't let you decide my life for me this way."

"Oh, yes you will! And so help me God, April, if you fight me now, I'll kidnap you."

"You and your grandfather! You're arrogant and macho and . . ."

"And what else?" His eyes had a dangerous glint.

". . . and I love you so much, I would have died if you'd left me."

"I'll never leave you, *gringa.*" He kissed her gently. "And you're right, I am arrogant and macho. I'll try to boss you and run your life and I'll scream like hell when you fight me. But I'll always love you, April. Always."

He put his arms around her and held her close. "There's something else we have to discuss."

"I wasn't aware what we just had was a discussion," she said.

Alejandro grinned, then kissed her again and said against her lips, "I'm going to have a hell of a time keeping you in line and trying to make a good Spanish wife out of you."

"Do you want me to be a good Spanish wife?"

He sighed and kissed the corner of her mouth. "No, *gringa*. I want you just the way you are. Now, will you please stop looking at me with those great cinnamon eyes of yours so I can get on with what we have to talk about?"

"Your profession," she said. "Yes, you're right, we *do* have to talk about it."

"April, I—"

"Okay. I hate it. It terrifies me. I know you can't understand my fear, but—"

"You're wrong, April. I do understand. Because of Rafa. When he's in the ring, I'm terrified too. I understand now how my mother felt and how you feel, but—"

"But you can't change the way you are."

"Not right away." He took a deep breath. "What I'm going to do—what *we're* going to do—is complete the South American and the Mexican tour. I've contracted for that and I never welsh on a contract. And I've got contracts here in Spain for another year and a half when we come back from South America."

April waited, her eyes on his face, feeling a quickening of her pulse, a glimmer of something she barely dared to hope for.

"When I complete my contracts . . ."

April knew what he was going to say. And suddenly she was afraid. For him. For what he might give up because of her.

"It's your life," she whispered. "I know what it means to you. I know how good you are."

She put her arms around him, feeling hot tears squeeze between her eyelids, loving him so much that his pain became her pain. His loss became her loss.

He kissed her cheek, kissed away the tears before his mouth found hers. "I'll have you," he said when he let her go. "And we'll have La Esperanza. Hope. That's a good name, isn't it? Our hope, April. We're going to build it into the best brave-bull ranch in the world. And I'll manage Rafa's career, if he still wants to continue in the profession."

He smiled at her. "You won't mind having a fifteen-year-old son, will you?"

April laughed with a joy she hadn't known was possible. "Not as long as I can give him lots of brothers and sisters."

Alejandro's green Gypsy eyes warmed with love. "As many as you want," he said in a husky voice. "Starting now." Then, before April could protest, he bent down and lifted her off the sofa and carried her into the bedroom.

Silhouette Intimate Moments

Coming Next Month

The Amber Sky by Kristin James

When Valerie de la Portilla first met Ashe Harlan it didn't look as though they'd spend a future together. But beneath the stormy sky of San Cristobal, suspicious antagonists by day turned to lovers by night.

The Danvers Touch by Elizabeth Lowell

Cat Cochran took nothing from her wealthy ex-husband but a determination to earn her own way in the world. Yet no matter how successful she became, she still dreamed of warmth in the cold center of the night—a dream turned into reality by Travis Danvers.

Another Kind Of Love by Mary Lynn Baxter

For Ali Cameron work was her only priority until she met Adam Forrest. He awoke emotions and sensations in her that she thought she'd never feel again. But was that enough to break the bonds of her old life and allow her to embrace the new?

The Gentle Winds by Monica Barrie

Jase Patten swept into Ti Caissen's orderly life like a cool wind. But there were rules to life in the valley—rules that said their love could never be. Yet how could they deny a love that grew stronger with each passing moment?

Silhouette
Intimate 💑 *Moments*

more romance, more excitement

Special Introductory Offer $1⁷⁵ each

#1 ☐ DREAMS OF EVENING
Kristin James

#3 ☐ EMERALDS IN THE DARK
Beverly Bird

#2 ☐ ONCE MORE WITH
FEELING Nora Roberts

#4 ☐ SWEETHEART CONTRACT
Pat Wallace

$2.25 each

#5 ☐ WIND SONG
Parris Afton Bonds

#11 ☐ UNTIL THE END OF TIME
June Trevor

#6 ☐ ISLAND HERITAGE
Monica Barrie

#12 ☐ TONIGHT AND ALWAYS
Nora Roberts

#7 ☐ A DISTANT CASTLE
Sue Ellen Cole

#13 ☐ EDGE OF LOVE
Anna James

#8 ☐ LOVE EVERLASTING
Moëth Allison

#14 ☐ RECKLESS SURRENDER
Jeanne Stephens

9 ☐ SERPENT IN PARADISE
Stephanie James

#15 ☐ SHADOW DANCE
Lorraine Sellers

#10 ☐ A SEASON OF
RAINBOWS Jennifer West

#16 ☐ THE PROMISE OF
SUMMER Barbara Faith

SILHOUETTE INTIMATE MOMENTS, Department IM/5
1230 Avenue of the Americas
New York, NY 10020

Please send me the books I have checked above. I am enclosing
$_____ (please add 50¢ to cover postage and handling. NYS
and NYC residents please add appropriate sales tax.) Send check or
money order—no cash or C.O.D.'s please. Allow six weeks for delivery.

NAME _____

ADDRESS _____

CITY _____ STATE/ZIP _____

Dear Reader:
Please take a few moments to fill out this questionnaire. It will help us give you more of the Silhouette Intimate Moments you'd like best.

Mail to: **Karen Solem**
Silhouette Books
1230 Ave. of the Americas, New York, N.Y. 10020

1. How did you obtain **THE PROMISE OF SUMMER?** `9-16`

10-1 ☐ **Bookstore**　　　　　　-6 ☐ **Newsstand**
　-2 ☐ **Supermarket**　　　　　-7 ☐ **Airport**
　-3 ☐ **Variety/discount store**　-8 ☐ **Book Club**
　-4 ☐ **Department store**　　　-9 ☐ **From a friend**
　-5 ☐ **Drug store**　　　　　　-0 ☐ **Other:**_____
　　　　　　　　　　　　　　　　　　　　　　(write in)

2. How many Silhouette Intimate Moments have you read including this one?
   (circle one number) 11- **1 2 3 4 5 6 7 8 9 10 11 12 13 14 15 16**

3. Overall how would you rate this book?
12-1 ☐ **Excellent**　-2 ☐ **Very good**
　-3 ☐ **Good**　-4 ☐ **Fair**　-5 ☐ **Poor**

4. Which elements did you like best about this book?
13-1 ☐ **Heroine**　-2 ☐ **Hero**　-3 ☐ **Setting**　-4 ☐ **Story line**
　-5 ☐ **Love scenes**　-6 ☐ **Ending**　-7 ☐ **Other Characters**

5. Do you prefer love scenes that are
14-1 ☐ **Less explicit than**　　　　-2 ☐ **More explicit than**
　　　in this book　　　　　　　　　　**in this book**
　　　　　　-3 ☐ **About as explicit as in this book**

6. What influenced you most in deciding to buy this book?
15-1 ☐ **Cover**　-2 ☐ **Title**　-3 ☐ **Back cover copy**
　-4 ☐ **Recommendations**　-5 ☐ **You buy all Silhouette Books**

7. How likely would you be to purchase other Silhouette Intimate Moments in the future?
16-1 ☐ **Extremely likely**　　　-3 ☐ **Not very likely**
　-2 ☐ **Somewhat likely**　　　-4 ☐ **Not at all likely**

8. Do you prefer books at (check one)
17-1 ☐ **A longer length of 256 pages?**　-3 ☐ **Other:**_____
　-2 ☐ **A shorter length of 192 pages?**　　　**(write in)**

9. Will **INTIMATE MOMENTS** affect your purchasing **SILHOUETTE DESIRES?** 18-1 ☐ **yes**　-2 ☐ **no**

---

10. Please check the box next to your age group.
19-1 ☐ **Under 18**　-3 ☐ **25-34**　　-5 ☐ **50-54**
　-2 ☐ **18-24**　　-4 ☐ **35-49**　　-6 ☐ **55 +**

11. Would you be interested in receiving a romance newsletter? If so please fill in your name and address.

Name_____

Address_____

City_____ State_____ Zip_____

19___20___21___22___23___